LONGNECKS & TWISTED HEARTS

A Bill Travis Mystery

GEORGE WIER

Published by
Flagstone Books
Austin, Texas

Longnecks & Twisted Hearts—*A Bill Travis Mystery*

First Print Edition
January 2013

ISBN-13: 978-1481109093
ISBN-10: 148110909X

The Bill Travis Mysteries:

The Last Call
Capitol Offense
Longnecks & Twisted Hearts

LONGNECKS & TWISTED HEARTS

A Bill Travis Mystery

DEDICATION

For Sallie, as always.

PROLOGUE

The French ship ran toward the lowering sun. Behind her, south-eastward, perhaps forty nautical miles distant, the wall of slate gray pursued: Hurricane.

The marauder's master emerged from his cabin, tromped up the companionway steps to the pilot deck and raised his glass.

They had been running before the storm for a week; as if it were a bloody hunt and themselves the prey.

"Capitan," his commander called to him. "There is land."

The Captain turned, raised his glass and peered through it. There *was* land: it was the familiar long and narrow strip of sand bar that an earlier Spanish explorer had named Corpus Christi, which meant "Body of Christ", perhaps for the fact of his deliverance from just such a storm as followed. Spaniards were superstitious. Louis considered that it was almost a form of blasphemy itself to go around naming things after Deity. Still... He turned back toward the distant wall of gray. If there was, truly, a personage — Deity himself — then he might be angry at Louis and his ship for the theft, if not the murders.

For the last six days the storm had tracked the ship and men across the Gulf of Mexico, as if consciously following every turn of the pilot. It was enough to make a man superstitious.

The day before the storm appeared, Louis du Orly and his crew had sacked a galleon on the Spanish Main, just off the coast of the island named for the order of friars who now inhabited it: Dominica.

They had taken five huge crates from the hold of the Spanish ship, each crate containing a treasure trove of gold and gems, and then they had burned the ship to the waterline. Now, belowdecks, Louis had a dozen papists — the survivors of his conquest — in chains. He would return them to France for use in an exchange of prisoners. Perhaps his old Captain himself could be returned to him.

But the storm — some of his men thought it was the Wrath of God himself — pursued. And France was so far away.

"Bear north," he called. "Head for Matagorda. We will take shelter on the *Brazos de Dios.*" In the Latin tongue it meant "The Arms of God", but in truth it was little more than a wide, muddy river that emptied into the Gulf of Mexico, named such by that idiot LaSalle. The story was that LaSalle, pursued by Indians, had stumbled upon the river, at first believing he had found the Mississippi. He swam it, and upon the other side he sank to his knees and offered a prayer to Divinity for delivering him, thus consecrating the river in God's name. The Indians, more worldy-wise, had not attempted the crossing. Perhaps they were not mere savages. Perhaps *they* were wise. The Brazos was treacherous. If stories were true, half as many as had attempted the crossing had not made it. There were tales of great eddies in the current that would swallow any craft lesser than a large sailing ship. Also, there were great beasts; reptiles up to thirty feet in length that could eat a man whole. A year before, Louis had taken *Le Royale* up-river perhaps ten miles and there had observed a great geyser of water and sand. As he brought his ship nearer, he observed a thing that was part fish and part reptile slink into the water and disappear. Through the course of his life Louis had found that legends, by and large, were not true. However, such stories were usually based upon some fact — some thing, however idiotic, and usually mis-observed. He would not himself have believed the animal existed had he not seen it. Yes, the Brazos was treacherous. But there was greater danger from sandbars, from the Indians, from disease and ignorance than there was from legendary dragons.

The Brazos was the only navigable river within range. It was his only option.

The storm followed them, as if driven by a diabolical intelligence. An intelligence with a taste for revenge.

Perhaps Satan, then. Louis could never bring himself to put his faith in a benevolent Deity. A malevolent one, though, was more realistic given the nature of life. Regardless, he would have to drive *Le Royale* far up-river to escape, and all the while the storm would be bearing down hard upon them. Sailing up-river through the meandering channel would take time, and time was a luxury he could ill afford.

It was the year of the Christian Savior 1673. The whole world was being swallowed up by Christianity, or so it seemed. Louis had narrowly escaped heresy charges himself by going to sea at the age of fifteen. His parents had been Huguenots, both slaughtered during the Purge when he was just a lad of eight. He had grown up under the uncertain guidance of his mother's brother.

Louis had been outspoken and willful. He did not believe in the Christian God, and had forever refused to take part in worship. He was one of a select few who had no God except his own ability to make his way in the world and do more than survive; Louis du Orly would commit the greatest blasphemy of all: he would flourish and prosper or die in the attempt. Thus far in his life he had found no middle ground between these two extremes.

From the seaport at Brest he entered the merchant employ of a garrulous shop-keeper, Simone Le Blanc, who while engendering Louis' loyalty would later sell his contract to a trading company that was set to sail for the New World.

And here he was, a hold laden with the ripest fruit of the New World — *gold* — and he was running like the coward he was certain his men now thought him to be.

"Monsieur Le Fitte," he called to his mate.

"Capitan?"

"I am about to do something. Something untried. If any ill befalls me, you are to take command."

"Oui," the young man replied, fear etched into his features. "What are you going to do?"

"I am going to make a pact with the Devil," Louis said. He turned from the quizzical gaze of his officer and looked toward the sandbar.

They were short of the bay by perhaps a hundred miles.

His eyes tracked back to the storm.

It would be close. Far too close.

He was twenty-five years old now, and had spent the last seven years of his life terrorizing the Spanish on the high seas. His *Lettres de Marque* gave him license in the name of the King to burn, pillage, and sack the Spaniards' ships. Just now the Dutch and the English, aside from his own shipmates, were his only friends.

Louis smiled and turned his eyes from the coming hurricane toward the steps down into his ship. He shut the gentle salt breeze outside behind him and plunged into the darkness belowdecks.

There on his desk was the chest, its gold framework limned with a shimmer of dying sunlight from the port window.

It had taken him days to work out the intricate lock. The pick tools, most of them garnered from among the crew, lay scattered across the desk. From memory he made quick work of the lock, and at the small *snik* sound, lifted the lid.

It lay inside upon a tiny mattress of fleece.

He reached in and withdrew the cold object and turned it about in his hands, his eyes roving over it, looking for any seam, any mark that might betray its maker or its manner of manufacture. There was none.

The object was in the shape of a wish-bone, no more than twenty inches high, and heavier than any normal metal, including gold itself. He had discovered its purpose by accident on their third day of flight from the storm. It had been beneath his coat, its bluish, smooth metal against his shirt, when he went down into the hold to inspect the treasure.

Before he could remove his key from his breeches, he felt the tugging.

This object of the Aztecs was pulling toward the door, as if it hungered. It came free of his shirt and pressed hard against the inner lining of his coat, tugging, shifting.

Louis had backed away from the hold door carefully, and as he did the tugging diminished, slowly. "Gold," he had thought. "It hungers for gold."

Later, sitting at his desk, he had watched the closed chest that contained the object. He had waited and thought on it while he waited.

If word of the thing were to spread among the Spaniards, they would come for him. They would track him to the ends of the Earth and seize it.

And it *had* whispered to him that same terrible night: *I hunger, Louis.*

Later that night he had awakened from a fevered dream and stood for an hour regarding the chest, waiting for it to speak again.

And now, this day, with the hurricane almost on top of them and the men in fear, Louis du Orly reversed himself along the passageway and emerged again upon the deck.

He strode to the foredeck of the ship. The men there stopped their work to watch him.

Louis du Orly lifted the object to the sky.

Overhead the slate gray clouds banked as if they were a mountain about to tumble down upon them. They heaved forward each passing moment with the weight of the great storm behind them.

"Hear me!" he du Orly cried. "Hear me, Storm. Hear me, God. Hear me, Satan!"

The men stood still, their mouths open and their eyes wide as their captain shouted towards the sky.

"I command you to deliver us!"

The lightning bolt flicked to him faster than the eye could travel. It danced and wove through the object, his arms, his brain, and then exited his left boot.

He fell, and knew no more.

*****

Louis du Orly awoke with a metallic taste in his mouth and a powerful thirst.

He sat bolt upright from his bed. Outside, the wind howled and the rain peppered the port window.

Le Fitte was by his side.

"Where are we?" Louis asked.

"On the Brazos de Dios."

"Safe?"

"The hurricane is here. We have lost two men."

"How long? How long was I asleep?"

"Three days."

"Three?"

"Oui. I feared for your life."

The ship swayed and rocked, driven hard by the wind and rain. Louis tried to sit, but his lieutenant pushed him gently back down.

"Rest, Capitan. Please. We will need you, if we are to survive this."

Louis nodded and laid his throbbing head back onto his feather pillow.

"How far? How far up-river?" he asked.

"A hundred miles. Possibly more."

"Impossible," Louis exclaimed.

"We have not once had to tack against the wind. The river is wide and deep and the way has been clear. It is a miracle sent from — It is a miracle."

"Where? Where is the blue bone?" Louis asked.

"In the chest."

Louis' eyes turned toward the table, and as he did, a lance of sheer pain went through his skull. The chest was there.

"Locked?" he asked.

"Even so."

Louis felt unaccountably tired. His strength ebbed away quickly. He gripped his lieutenant's hand, fought to gather his thoughts to say something, something important, he felt, but as he grasped for it, it fled.

And darkness descended upon him again.

"Rest, mon Capitan," Le Fitte said.

Du Orly snored softly.

CHAPTER ONE

It seems there is never a good time for anything to happen in life, good or bad.

For instance, I was in a courtroom about to hear the closing arguments in a lawsuit between a friend of mine and the guy who had rooked him out of a neat hundred-thousand bucks when I got the word that my best friend from childhood had been killed.

Bradley Fisher and I had known each other from second grade straight on through. I never had a brother, but if I had I don't know that he could have been any closer to me than Brad had been. Once.

I'd had a feeling of intense wrongness from the moment my head hit the pillow the night before. That feeling had intensified in my dreams and I awakened covered in a cold sweat around three-fifteen in the morning, that time when the night seems to be its darkest and the hope of any light is a world removed. I read once that three-fifteen is the witching hour. I never knew any witches to confirm it, but still, it's an hour that's best slept through. Somehow I got back to sleep, nuzzling into the warm, slumbering cocoon that is my wife.

The trial resumed at nine as if the night had never occurred. But my usual slim breakfast turned into a ball of nervous lead around nine-thirty and despite the fact that I had my head in the very serious game that was unfolding before me, the sense that something, somewhere, had gone south stayed with me.

My pager vibrated.

I don't normally carry a cell phone or a pager, but Julie was scheduled to deliver at any time and if all went well I'd be a father.

Somehow I knew that the oppressive and disquieting feeling of wrongness had nothing to do with Julie or the baby.

I jumped in my seat. The vibration in my pants pocket felt like an electric shock — as if I'd touched a live wire. I fumbled in my pants pocket, attempting to look nonchalant.

A row ahead of me, just past the inlaid wood barrier between the public and the court, my friend looked over at me with a puzzled expression on his face. I used my face to try to convey a shrug. It worked. He nodded once, giving me an "Okay."

The 979 prefix on my pager told me at once that the number was from back home — Bryan, Texas, my hometown, or at least within the same area code.

My throat went dry.

It was Brad's home phone number.

The judge looked at me. He had a practiced, concerned look on his face.

I shook my head: Nothing.

"I gotta go," I whispered.

The Judge nodded.

*****

"Hello?" It was Brad's wife Mary Jo who answered the phone.

"Mary Jo. It's Bill."

"Oh God, Bill. Brad's dead."

I felt the blood drain out of my head. Suddenly I was leaning against the smooth travertine blocks that made up one of the walls outside the court room. I tried to say something, but I had no breath.

"Bill, I'm so sorry —" Mary Jo choked down into heavy sobs.

Somehow I managed to breathe.

"What happened?" I asked.

"I knew they were going to kill him. I tried to tell him. But Brad doesn't — didn't listen to me."

"Mary Jo. It's not your fault. Brad never listened to anybody."

It was true.

I recalled an instance where Brad hadn't listened. Back around early 1990 Brad had called me up in a frenzy to get me in on the ground floor with him in what would later be called the junk bond market. He invested eighty thousand dollars, the bulk of his inheritance from his father, and sat back and waited for it to turn into a cool million. I did my best to warn him off of it without making him wrong or thoroughly raining on his parade. I'd wanted him to hold back. To try ten thousand first, or maybe five. He wasn't having any of it. I'm not even sure he heard me. There are no dreams quite like golden dreams — money falling from the sky like pennies from heaven. And there was no way that Brad was going to let the dream walk on by.

When the bottom fell out of the junk bond market I called him up, hoping that I wasn't too late. I'd had the disturbing image in my mind of my best friend holding a gun to his head and pulling the trigger. But Brad was all right. It was okay for me to breathe easy. You live and you learn. "Don't ever worry about me, Bill," he had said. "I'll always be here."

Except he wasn't. Not anymore.

"Bill?" Mary Jo said. I could hear the concern in her voice. She'd just lost her husband and here she was worried about me.

"Don't worry about me, Mary Jo," I told her.

"That's what Brad always told me. Don't repeat him, Bill."

"Okay," I said. "I'll try not to. But it's hard."

"Bill, I know who did this. I know who killed him."

"Okay, Mary Jo. I'm coming. Right now."

*****

Outside the Travis County Courthouse I walked the block over to where I parked my Mercedes during the trial. Along the way I called Julie.

"How you feeling, Darlin'?" I asked her.

"I'm fine. Why aren't you in the trial?"

"Baby, I just got some bad news. My old running buddy, Bradley Fisher — his wife paged me while I was in Court. Brad's dead."

"She called me and I gave her your pager number," she said. "She didn't sound so good but she wouldn't tell me anything."

"I was wondering how she got my number."

"She just said it was an emergency. I'm sorry, Baby," she said. "Are you going to be okay?"

I thought about it. I suppose I had to be.

"I'll be all right. It's a bit of a shock, is all. Brad and I have been drifting apart for some years."

"And now he's gone," she said.

"Yeah."

"You need to take off, don't you?" I could hear it in her voice — the certainty of someone who knows me like no other could.

The baby was due any time. I couldn't not be there by her side when the time came, whenever that was.

"Bill?"

"I'm here," I said.

"I'll be fine," she said, reading my mind, as always. "Go, okay? Just go."

"I've got to be here when you deliver," I said, my throat feeling dry.

"You will be. Just no more hanging from blimps, no more shootouts. You got that?"

"Baby. We don't even own a gun."

"I know. But somehow guns seem to find you."

"Yeah," I said. She was right. "I know."

"How did he die?"

"Mary Jo told me that somebody killed him and that she knows who did it. Beyond that, it's why I'm going. I simply don't know."

"And you need to."

"Need to know?" I asked, but then realized Julie was anticipating me, as usual. "Yeah. I suppose I have to."

CHAPTER TWO

There's an old saying: "You can't put your foot into the same river twice." Time is like that. You turn around and look where you were looking just a few seconds before, and something will have changed, just in that short interval.

With my home town the change this time was bone deep, and while my toes hadn't been back in these waters for some time, still I was expecting... well, *home.*

I'd passed through the burgh a few times in my comings and goings across Texas in the years since I left high school. During those previous infrequent trips I had noted that other than the new civic buildings, the new strip malls and retail outlets, and the obvious expansion outward into areas of the county that I had once considered the untracked wilderness, the changes had been superficial. It was the same town. There had once been a Perry's Department Store on Bryan Street — gone now. But the Dairy Queen still doled out the ice cream and "Hunger-Buster" hamburgers, and the Baptists still had the market cornered on the local soul harvest. In these respects all was right with the world because home was, to this degree, still home.

But then a very unhome-like event occurred.

Red and blue flashed in my rearview mirror.

I was being pulled over.

Fine, I thought. *Welcome back.*

"License and registration, please," the policeman said. He had a stone face. I was willing to bet he'd spent hours at a time practicing it in a mirror until he had it perfect. You could have used a chisel on his face and broken the thing.

"Sure," I said. I fished out my license and the registration and handed them over to him with a calculated nonchalance.

He took them, glanced at the registration and stood unmoving, looking at my driver's license.

"I'm from Austin," I said. "My best friend died and I'm in town to pay my respects."

"My condolences," the policeman said. If he meant it then I had complete lack of insight into human character.

"Say," I said. "Why'd you stop me? Did I do anything wrong?"

"Ran a red light," he said, trying to drill little holes into me with his eyes.

"I turned right on red. I came to a complete stop. Looked, then turned. Not trying to argue or anything, but you know that's what happened."

"You don't know anything that I know," he said.

He looked back down at my license.

"Is this your correct address?" the policeman asked, his eyes moving back and forth from me to my driver's license.

"Yes," I said. I normally reserve "sir" for people I have actually found respectable, or for dignitaries like the Governor. Thus far I'd found nothing about the guy to respect.

"Travis, William. Wait here, William."

"It's Bill," I said. I looked at his name tag. It read "H. Leonard."

"Bill, huh? Are there any other assumed names you answer to?"

"No, Officer Leonard," I said. "It's not an assumed name, it's *my* name. Bill — William. William — Bill. Like Hank for Henry." I yawned. Yawning usually works best with his kind.

"I know what a nickname is. Any other assumed names, Bill?"

"No," I said. I was long past tired of the guy.

"Wait here."

I waited.

He was in his cruiser behind me for all of ten minutes. I glanced in my rearview mirror from time to time. What the hell was he doing?

Officer Leonard returned.

"Mr. Travis," he said, handing me my license and registration. I took them. "I'm going to do you a favor."

I didn't even have to think about it. "That's not necessary," I said.

"Still, you're going to accept this favor."

"Okay, what is it?"

"You're going to start up your car. You will turn right at the next intersection. You will turn right again at the very next stop sign. When you come to the next stop sign you will turn left. You will proceed back in the direction from whence you came, not deviating. I will follow you until you have crossed the Brazos River Bridge from Brazos County over into Burleson County. Go back to Austin, Mr. Travis."

"You're running me out of town, huh? Why?"

He leaned toward me.

"Mr. Travis. I firmly believe that you would be better off not exploring the alternative."

"Fine," I said, not missing a beat.

It's an eighteen-mile drive through relatively flat river-bottom countryside west from Bryan to the wide and muddy waters of the Brazos River.

In the last two miles I had to restrain myself from speeding. My toes itched.

Also, I was hopping mad.

I thought about Brad and about Mary Jo; Brad as I had remembered him with a toothy grin on his craggy face, and Mary Jo as I would probably find her, trying to smile and be her warm and courteous self even as the tears rolled down her face.

As I approached the bridge I glanced up in my rearview. Officer H. Leonard slowed down and moved off the road. Probably he'd sit there for a good half hour or more and wait to see if I turned back around and crossed again.

Fine, I thought.

I've been known to be a tad single-minded. Some might call it stubbornness.

Two miles down the road I took the turn-off south onto a highway that I knew followed the course of the river for fifteen miles to a four-way stop. I rolled down that highway pushing ninety-five. A left at the four-way and I was back in College Station, Bryan's twin city.

There was more than one way to come home.

CHAPTER THREE

I was back home and beginning to seethe a little less.

I made a quick cell phone call and got Julie. She was fine. She didn't want me to worry about her. Do what I had to do, stay for the funeral if I needed to and for as many days as I needed after that, then get back to Austin. I told her I'd try to commute back and forth as needed. She loved me. I loved her. The baby was taking her time. I could understand it. If that were me in there, I wouldn't want to leave either.

I passed by Texas A&M University, which had now spread itself out into the old cow pastures west of the main campus, and the college appeared to be bursting at the seams. Not that there was ever a time it wasn't.

A campus policeman passed by me. I looked down at my speedometer. I was just under the limit. We ignored each other, and that was a good thing.

I turned and skirted the campus heading south and paralleling the railroad tracks and the main campus loomed on my left. College kids crossed the road on foot and bicycle, not even looking up at the traffic.

I may have been watching for all the changes in the city of my rearing, but I was also attempting to avoid certain painful thoughts.

There is nothing like losing someone close to you to remind you of your own mortality. I'm not usually a morose fellow. I'm generally too busy to take notice that the days, months and years are flitting past me. That's how I've always lived: stay busy, keep moving, and stick to the program.

Lately, for me, the program had been not engaging every little invitation to disaster that came rampaging my way. Me, I'm a mild-mannered financial consultant. Well, maybe not so mild-mannered, at least according to my wife. It was the world of trouble outside my insular little world that seemed to want to bust my door down, and far too often. The previous fall, I'd had a run-in with a latent insurgent Republic of Texas revolutionary group that had come very close to assassinating the Governor of Texas. Somehow I'd gotten out alive. I don't know how I did. About all I can say is that I was still breathing afterwards.

The last few miles to Brad and Mary Jo's house I spent introspectively, thinking about the ghosts of good times past, and more than a few not-so-good times.

I thought about Brad. I'd known him since the two of us were kids. There was one occasion that usually sprang up when I thought very long on the subject of Brad. When we were kids we used to pick up extra spending money by shoveling horse manure at a quarter-horse stable near my family home. We mucked out stables and kept the horses watered and put them on the walker — all sorts of things. The time I was thinking about, Brad wanted to ride an old brood mare named Daisy — a horse that us kids had not-so-affectionately renamed "Hell Bitch." That day Hell Bitch was fine during the curry-combing and hoof-cleaning, didn't nip at us with her huge teeth as we put a blanket on her and cinched a saddle into place. But the instant that Brad got in the saddle, she took off.

He tried to rein her in, but she was too much horse for him. He ended up getting pitched off at a full gallop right onto a barbed-wire fence.

It wasn't pretty. I had thought at the time that he was a goner. Before his ride I had entertained the notion that I might ride Hell Bitch. After that, we mutually agreed to give her a wide berth. Daisy didn't get much grooming after Brad's run-in with the fence. All told it took twenty-six stitches to put him back together interspersed between his left clavicle, his right arm, and a spot just below his belt but thankfully above his groin. As I saw it he wasn't just lucky to have kept his baby-making packaging — he was fortunate to still be able to breathe, or what's more, walk.

As many rough scrapes and tight places as I had been in, Brad had me beat by about a factor of ten.

And there I was all of a sudden — pulling into his driveway.

Bradley wasn't home. He would never be home again

CHAPTER FOUR

All of Mary Jo's tears had dried, and seeing me at her front door did not at once set her off again. She hugged me, squeezing me tightly.

"Bill, you're the first one here," she said.

"Who else is coming?"

"Brad's brother, Freddie. That's about it for now, as Brad's parents are dead and it was just the boys."

"Sure. I remember Freddie. We never got along, though."

"I know," she said.

I followed Mary Jo into the house. The place had not changed much since they were married. It was her house. Mary Jo had a little money of her own. She was frugal with every dime that came her way; a complete opposite from Brad in that respect, but in all others they matched up fine.

She took me into the kitchen, chattering all the way, avoiding the main topic.

"Coffee?" she asked.

"Yes," I said. "Lots."

"Good." The coffee was already made. Probably she'd done it out of habit. Brad usually had a cup when he came home from work. She poured two cups and set them down by me at her kitchen table. I watched the steam boil off of it.

She sat down at my right elbow, crossed her arms on the table and looked at me. She had such beautiful eyes, and right then they were full of inexpressible sadness and grief. I didn't know whether to grab her and hold her or start crying myself. She was such a fine woman. I hoped that Brad knew what he was leaving behind.

"Mary Jo, who killed Brad?" I asked after a few unbearable minutes.

She almost lost it for a moment. She bit her bottom lip and held her head erect. I could tell she was fighting to keep it together, and doing a damn fine job of it.

"Officially, it was an accident," she said, her voice clipping off the words.

"Tell me what happened."

"Bradley told me a week ago that if anything happened to him that he wanted me to pack my bags, put up a For Sale sign on the house and run off to Florida, or Maine, or anyplace but here. He knew, Bill."

I waited.

"He knew. I didn't want to believe him at first, but I saw that he had changed. He never smiled anymore. He never laughed..."

"Mary Jo," I said. "If someone hurt Brad, I need to know who and how."

"I wanted to call you. I told Brad I was going to. He got mad. It was the first time he ever raised his voice to me. He told me 'No!' emphatically. I was not to call you no matter what."

And then she did it. She broke down, burying her head in her enfolded arms on the kitchen table. I wanted to reach out to her, to touch her and reassure her. But there was no reassurance I could give. I made out the words "should have" and "why didn't I" amidst her sobs.

"Mary Jo," I said, pressing gently.

"It's my fault," she sobbed the words out.

"No," I told her. "You could never have hurt Brad. It's not in your nature."

I let her go on, wishing all the while that I could be a thousand miles away. I don't like to see a woman cry. Through hard experience, however, I have discovered that it's always best to let a person feel what they're feeling. It's when you resist it that real problems develop.

She wiped her eyes on her sweater.

"He was running a work crew," she began. "Not the crew he had trained, but a different crew. He hated his job, and I hated that he kept working at a job that he hated, but I could never tell him anything, you know? Yeah. You do know." She picked up her coffee cup and sipped at it. I followed her example. It was good coffee.

"From what Mike Fields tells me — he was the only guy at CTL&P that Brad trusted — Brad got hit with about ten thousand volts when he went into a satellite station that had detected a power drain. Other than that, I don't know. They won't let me see his body, Bill."

I got an unpleasant image in my head. A picture of Brad's body convulsing as his clothes and skin and hair caught on fire. I shook my head, trying to wipe the image out of existence.

"Mary Jo, there might not be much of his body left."

She looked up at me, her eyes wide open now and aware.

"I know," she said. "But until I see something, none of this will be real."

"Yeah. I know," I told her. "Who wanted to kill Brad?"

"Why, the company, of course."

*****

Brad had gone to work for Central Texas Light and Power some fifteen years before. He had worked his way up to foreman after two years, then to supervisor. I was never sure how the chain of command worked in such outfits, but I knew that Brad's only having a high school diploma had kept him from rising to the very top. I knew — and certainly Mary Jo and Brad himself knew — that he knew more about engineering than the professors in college who taught the courses. But also I knew that in this country it's the sheepskin that counts. It's paper that, in the final analysis, is more important than people. You can't even die properly unless your paperwork is done.

It took a little longer to drag the rest of the story out of Mary Jo.

From what I gathered, Brad had never given her a "why." What she was able to tell me was a "who." A name. The guy who ran the show over at CTL&P.

When she first told me the name it stirred some of the cobwebbed furniture around in the back of my mind — that place reserved for almost useless yet unpleasant memories.

Terry Throckmorton, she had told me.

The name was familiar to me, but at the moment I couldn't place it. Couldn't get a face to go with it, nor connect it up directly with any single event from my former life in that town. But it was significant, and I felt an old, familiar chill coming home to roost in my stomach.

I asked her if she felt like she was in danger, if she needed to take some measures — lock up the house and get out of Dodge for a while as Brad had suggested.

The answer was "No." There would still be a memorial service, even if the locals wouldn't give up Brad's body in time for a proper funeral. There was Brad's brother to think about, and his friends, like me. Come hell or high water she would give him a proper send off.

I found myself admiring her. Her fortitude and pluck.

"Do you have any protection here?" I asked her.

"I've got Brad's shotgun behind the front door and a pistol in my top dresser drawer. I think both are loaded." She looked at me. "I know how to shoot, Bill."

"Oh. All right. But shooting and killing are two different things."

"My father took me hunting with him when I was growing up. I think he wanted a boy, but what he got was me. If I can kill an innocent deer, I can kill a man trying to kill *me*."

"Good," I said. "I hate the idea of you being alone just now, but I've got to go."

"Where are you going?" she asked me.

"I need to talk to Mike Fields."

"Oh," she said. "I forgot to tell you. I told Mike that Brad's best friend was coming from Austin."

"Why did you tell him, Mary Jo, if you think he's involved in Brad's... uh, case?"

"I had to tell him *who* was coming, Bill. I wanted to scare him."

"Why should he be afraid of me?" I asked.

"You'll see," she said.

I held her screen door open, one foot on the front porch and one inside the front door.

"How well do you know Mike?" I asked her.

"He's been over for barbecues more than a few times. And just about every time that Brad got distracted for more than a minute, Mike would hit on me."

She easily read the expression on my face.

"No, Bill. I'd never do that. And I didn't. I wasn't attracted to him anyway. I'd never hurt Brad. He and Brad would usually get into a contest to see who could kill the most longnecks in an evening. Brad usually won."

"Does Mike know anyone at the police department over in Bryan?"

"Well... Yes. I think so. I think his father is the Chief of Police."

CHAPTER FIVE

I like things nice and neat. For some reason I never seem to get them that way.

First, somebody didn't want me in town, and given the information I'd just gotten from Mary Jo, that person was either Mike Fields or his father, the Chief of Police. Second was the fact that neither Mary Jo nor I had seen Brad's body. I put that about number two on the agenda.

So first was to drop in on Mike Fields, Brad's longneck buddy.

*****

Mike Fields and I had a bit of a history. In junior high and high school he'd been a bully, the kind who kicks kids' chairs out from under them in the cafeteria or who goes out of his way to find the geekiest kid around and cajole him into taking a swing at him and then punching the kid's lights out. When I was in my mid- and late-teens, I had an average build and quick wit. Also, I'd taken kick-boxing lessons for a full summer between eighth and ninth grade just for the hell of it, so I had enough confidence to stand my ground when guys like Mike came around. One evening I found myself waiting for my father to pick me up after school. There was no one else around until I turned to see Mike leaning against a low concrete wall not thirty feet away.

"What're you looking at?" he asked me.

"I just wanted to see what a class clown looks like outside of class," I replied.

"What's that supposed to mean?" he asked, shifting forward into a fast walk in my direction.

"Just a little IQ test," I said. "I wanted to see if you knew when you were being insulted. Looks like you passed."

His walk turned into a run. I stood there. At the last moment I stepped to the side, stuck my leg out, caught his back with a hard shove and watched him plow up ten inches of grass and sod with his face.

About that moment my father pulled into the parking lot.

I walked over and climbed inside the family car.

"What's his problem?" my dad asked me, gesturing towards Mike Fields, who was trying to gain his feet.

"Some people like to eat grass, I guess," I said.

"Oh," my dad replied.

*****

I stopped at a local Quicky-Mart, gassed up my Mercedes, and borrowed the store's phone book. Mike Fields had a listing. I jotted down the address, and even as I did, that action seemed familiar to me; as if I had written down the address before. A long time ago, maybe.

Back in the car, wending my way through familiar streets and main thoroughfares, I pegged the sensation that was gnawing at me. It was that Mike Fields lived on the upper middle-class side of Bryan on the exact street where a girl I had worshipped back in my high school days used to live. Back then, about the time I left Bryan for my first semester at Sam Houston State in Huntsville, I had persuaded myself that I'd never again find myself on Morning Glory Lane.

So much for that wish.

The sun was climbing down the back side of the sky and undulating shafts of fading sunlight played through willow and pin-oak trees and danced upon well-manicured lawns. I had arrived in the land of the status-conscious. There was a fine cool breeze blowing and I had the windows down on my old Mercedes.

I slowed and looked at a couple of mailboxes and front curbs with painted house numbers until I had a bearing on which side of the street the house was on and how far away it was.

I sailed down another two blocks.

Sure enough, it was the same house as my old high school flame. Hence the old rhetorical question, "What are the odds?"

There was an uneasy feeling in my gut.

I realized I was sweating, but it was a cold sweat.

*****

"Bill? Bill Travis?"

"Hello, Heidi."

"My God, I haven't seen you in... forever."

She looked good. There were tiny crow's-feet at the corners of her eyes, and she looked slightly more hollow than she had decades past, if that was possible. Back in high school she had been on the wispy side — just a thin slip of a girl and not "pretty" in the conventional sense. To a Byronic high school kid, namely yours truly, she had instead borne a sad beauty. Of course the woman before me was older than I remembered her, but the sadness was still there even as she smiled at me.

"Come in, Bill" she said.

"Are you Mrs. Fields now?" I asked her as she led me into the heart of her home.

When I was younger I had fantasized about being inside the place, had dreamed up furnishings and wall hangings and placed them just so. Heidi's home on the inside was nothing like what I had imagined.

"Yes. Do you know Mike? He never mentioned that he knew you," she said. "I would have remembered."

The Fields' tastes ran to nineteenth century antique. A large foxhunt mural hung in the living room area, a room that looked unlived in — a place to sit guests down and chat; nothing more. The furniture was imitation Queen Anne, enough to appear pretentious, if not uncomfortable. It was all crushed velvet and old leather and had an unused feel about it.

"Mike and I know each other." I said. "Heidi, do you remember Bradley Fisher?"

"God, yes. Mike told me about that. He and Brad were pretty close."

"How close?"

The question had the effect of a small slap.

"They were weekend drinking buddies. That's the only thing I never liked about their friendship. I'm not sure who was worse. I mean... who was the bad influence on whom, if you know what I mean. How's Mary Jo taking it?"

I took a seat on a tawny-colored leather sofa, and she sat across from me in a wing-backed chair. She crossed her legs. Heidi looked nice in form-fitting blue jeans and white sweater.

"About as well as can be expected," I told her. "Her husband is dead, and she thinks somebody killed him."

I waited. Let the news sink in.

Truth to tell, at one time I had been deeply in love with the woman in front of me. When a young man reaches the chasm that lies between adolescence and manhood he finds the gulf to be far wider and the depths to be far deeper and darker than he ever could have imagined. And smack dab in the middle of that narrow bridge is usually the ghostly figure of a young woman on her way to adulthood. But Heidi's bridge and my bridge never truly intersected. She had passed me by. Close, but nonetheless gone. Instead of befriending her I'd asked her out one fine day before lunch near the end of our junior year of high school. She demurred. I was crushed. I spent the next several months acting like a wounded hound dog, too pathetic to shoot and little good to anybody. Then, one day during the summer I woke up.

I had spent that summer between junior and senior year mowing lawns, edging around tombstones in outlying cemeteries with an old weedeater and hauling hay — anything to make an extra buck. By the time school rolled around again I had bought a car with my own money, had muscled up to fighting physique and bore a bronze tan from head to toe. I suppose when I returned to school that final year that I was something to behold. Also I had money in the bank.

When Heidi approached me that first day of school, obviously interested and wanting to talk, I ignored her and turned and walked away.

We spent that entire year ignoring each other's existence. We must have passed each other a thousand times in the hall with never a flicker of the eye in the other's general direction.

"About high school," I began, before she could respond further, "you do know how I felt about you, right? Before that last year."

Her head did the slightest little bobble, as if unconsciously. It was her eyes, though, that held my attention. The same sad blue eyes of the young and shy girl that I had enshrined as a sacred image for the better part of a lifetime, suspended as if frozen in liquid glass in my memory. There is no love quite like a first love.

"I knew, Bill. The whole world knew. You wore your heart on your sleeve."

Yeah. I supposed that she was right.

"We're both married now," I said.

"Yes, we are."

Was it me, or was the room getting warm?

I got a picture in my head. A picture of Julie, her face close to mine, looking into my eyes. When was that? Some hotel room a long time ago. Maybe it was right after we first met.

"You don't, anymore," Heidi said.

"What?"

"Wear your heart on your sleeve."

"Nope," I said. "Somebody else has the keeping of it."

And as the last syllable hung in the air between us, the front door opened.

Mr. Fields was home.

CHAPTER SIX

"Oh. Hello. And who might you be?" Mike Fields asked, and then a tenth of a second later recognized me.

"Mike, you remember Bill Travis? He's Brad's friend. He's here *about* Brad."

I stood, turned toward him, just as I had that day so long ago.

I found that after all the years intervening between our last meeting and this that I still didn't like Mike Fields, and the feeling was mutual.

His expression changed from surprise and puzzlement to shock and something else. His face began turning beet red. I was reminded of a bear that had been awakened too early before spring.

Mike Fields was a large, tall man. He had a good six inches on me and at least seventy pounds, and despite the fact that his gut stuck out a few inches over the top of his belt, I was sure he wasn't all fat. I got the image of an unstoppable mass if he was in a hurry, with the speed, force and pulsing red anger of a charging bull when he was furious. I was in his living room and there were breakable things about. Hopefully, with his wife there, I was safe.

Mike struck me as the kind of guy who didn't look forward to visitors, even despite the furnishings, and especially to visitors who'd once made him eat a patch of school lawn. I understood the sentiment. There is often a fine line between being a visitor and being a trespasser. As we stared at each other, I knew which category I had been relegated to.

Something Brad had told me once came back to me while I found myself returning my steady gaze to a man whose wife — once the object of my full, unrequited attentions — stood two feet to my left. Brad had said: “Mike’s the kind of guy that could go hunting with just his fists. That’s why I made friends with the guy.”

“Mike,” Heidi said. “Say something. Make it something nice.”

Mike began breathing again. He deflated, slowly.

“How’s Mary Jo doing?” he asked me.

It was my turn to be nice.

“She’s gonna be okay. I’ve just got to see her through the funeral. After that, life begins anew for her.”

“Yeah,” he said.

“When *is* the funeral?” Heidi asked. Mike dropped a well-worn suit jacket over the back of the sofa and came on into the living room. He didn’t bother to offer to shake hands. That was fine by me.

“Well,” I began. “There won’t be a proper funeral until Mary Jo gets the body.”

“Oh,” Mike said. “That.”

“Yeah. That.”

His eyes flicked toward me, then away.

“Is there some kind of a hold up?” Heidi asked.

“That’s why I’m here,” I said. “I was hoping to find out what I could from your husband before I go blundering into trouble.”

“Babe,” he said to Heidi. “Why don’t you rustle up some food?” Then to me: “Hot dogs and beer okay?”

“Perfect,” I said.

“We’ll be out back,” he told his wife.

She’d been given her marching orders and didn’t appear too put off by them. I followed Mike Fields out the sliding-glass patio door off their dining room and into a Japanese Tea Garden, the creation and maintenance of which must have set the Fields back a pretty penny.

"You know, Travis..." he began, but then trailed off.

"I know. You could break me in half. Let's call it quits on those days. We were both hotheads. Call me Bill."

"Bill," he said, testing the word and testing the waters at the same time. "Okay. We'll try first name basis, Bill."

"Fine, Mike," I said.

We sat down at a picnic table on the patio across from each other.

"Bill," he said. "I'm sure Mary Jo told you she thought Brad had been murdered. Also, you've no doubt learned that my father is the Chief of Police here, and you've probably put that together with being chased out of town."

"That was your doing," I said, knowing I was right.

"Damn right it was."

"Good," I said.

"What?"

"I can't stand a mystery."

"Oh. Well, now you know."

"Mike, I *know* diddly-squat. Which is why I'm here. Tell me a couple of things, will you."

"Like what?" he asked.

"About Brad. And trouble."

CHAPTER SEVEN

"You don't know what trouble is," he told me.

Each of us had a Shiner Bock longneck in our right hand, having been placed there by Heidi, whose timing was impeccable. When she disappeared back inside, the bull session resumed.

"Oh? I don't know about that," I said. "I think trouble is what we make it. I used to make a lot of it. You think I'm making it now?"

He thought about it for moment.

"No," he said. "But Bradley Fisher sure did. I tried to keep him from screwing up. He wasn't having any of it. Some people you can't help, you know? Now you, on the other hand. You're a smart fellow. Accountant, right?"

"Something like that. Right."

"Okay then. You know that there are some lines you don't cross. Some people you don't piss off."

I sat there, expressionless.

"Brad never met a line he couldn't or wouldn't cross."

"Who killed him?" I asked.

"See? There you go. I was hoping you were smarter than that."

"Mike. I need to know why my best friend's wife is a grieving widow. And if there are some powers that be who are responsible, you'd better tell who they are. And why."

"I don't better tell you a *goddamned* thing if I don't want to." He took a long draw on his bottle. I decided to use mine to keep my hand numb, at least for awhile. My hand wanted to make a fist.

"You're out of your depth," he continued after he set the bottle back down, two-thirds empty.

"How so?"

"You ought to feel privileged. You know, I come home and find *you* sitting talking with my wife. That was either real dumb or real smart. I can't pulverize you into dog meat while you're here because of her."

"Old Indian trick," I said.

"What?"

"Back in Old West days a white settler could walk into an Indian camp and expect food and drink and safety, even among his most bitter enemies."

"You're like Brad," Mike said. "Out of his depth. Never met a problem he didn't like."

"He was your friend?" I asked him.

"Yeah," he said.

"Mine too," I said. "There's no reason you and I can't be friends, then. That is, unless you had something to do with his early death."

"You two go back a ways, huh?" he asked.

I thought about it. I'd had maybe three or four real friends during my forty or so years on planet Earth. The oldest, longest, was Brad Fisher.

"He was my oldest friend," I told him. "What about you?"

He looked down at the table. The big man had small, twinkling eyes.

"Bill, I thought my crying days were dead and done."

I waited.

"But, when Terry Throckmorton gave me the word that Brad was dead —"

His face reddened before my eyes. Probably he had a bullfrog-sized lump in his throat. Moisture was there at the inner corners of his eyes.

I waited longer.

"Then I had to tell Mary Jo that Brad was... gone. And later when she called me back and told me you were coming to town... I figured there had been enough, uh, trouble for awhile."

"You were protecting me, then? By having me run out of town." I couldn't help the dubious tone of my words.

We both turned as the sliding glass door to the dining room moved back smoothly on its track. Heidi emerged again, this time with three longnecks. I could smell hotdogs cooking.

She set one in front of us each and put the third one down to the left of her husband and took a seat beside him.

"Don't worry. The hotdogs are on low heat. I'm joining you two for a moment," she said. Heidi looked at her husband as he turned to regard her. "Whether you like it or not," she said.

*****

"You two better start talking soon," she said after her first long draught from her bottle.

Mike and I had been sitting there staring at each other.

"Honey," Mike began.

"Don't 'Honey' me," she said. "Remember that I spent ten years teaching deaf kids. I can read lips when I have to."

Mike rolled his eyes.

Heidi had just the hint of a smirk at the corners of her mouth.

"That's the same as eavesdropping," Mike said. "But we'll talk about that later."

"It *is* the same and we *won't* be talking about it later. Bill, he married me because I was the first person he ever met who didn't take his blustery exterior. He's really just an overgrown kitten."

Somehow I doubted that, but I wasn't going to say it.

"You used your father to run Bill out of town and you won't tell him what really happened with Bradley Fisher. You two are sitting here like a couple of game cocks about to spur it out. That's bullshit! Mike, Bill is good people. You tell him what you know."

"And if I don't."

She turned toward him. Her eyes flashed. My God but I had never seen this side of her. I'd had this big illusion in my head about her ever since I was a kid. That illusion was gone now, shattered. Thank God.

"I think you don't want to test me on it," she said.

He sighed, big.

"No, I reckon I don't," he said. "Bill. I take it from your ring that you're married as well. Does your wife ever talk to you like that?"

"I never give her a reason to. But I'm sure she could if she felt she had to."

"Yeah," he said. He turned away from Heidi. "Okay. I'll tell you what you want to know. Who knows? Maybe when I'm done you'll get in your car and head back to Austin anyway. I know I would if I were you."

He tossed down the last dregs of his bottle and wrapped his big, meaty right hand around the next bottle in line.

While Heidi went to retrieve our supper, I listened to his story.

CHAPTER EIGHT

"You have to know how a company is put together, from the bottom all the way to the top, and you have to know a little bit about how people are put together as well, because that's what makes up a company, large or small. Now at the bottom and all the way in between you've got the little guy, slogging it out day in and day out, trying to do his job and survive in a world that would just as soon be rid of him as see him survive. In the scheme of things, little fish are supposed to remain little fish. But then there's the big fish. This guy swims in his own domain, and the little fish either get out of his way or get eaten up. That's where Terry Throckmorton comes in. You've got a guy there who's played the game ever since he was in college. When his frat senior said 'Jump', Terry didn't ask 'How high?' he just jumped as high as he could. And in his senior year he didn't bother to tell his juniors to jump, he was asking the Dean if he wanted somebody to jump for *him.* And so on after graduation and into the corporate world. In other words, we're talking about a guy who has paid his dues, and never stopped paying them just so long as the gravy train continued to stop and unload, stop and unload. The thing about that gravy train is it just keeps on unloading. All you have to do is let it know where to dump its load.

"And that's Terry Throckmorton, in a nutshell.

"Then you've got a guy like Bradley Fisher. Brad was small fish who always looked upon himself as a big fish that never quite made it into the big pond. Brad had ideas. Guys like Brad always have ideas. He had ideas about how to increase production, about how to make service easier and simpler. About how to cut back on the amount of labor and at the same time get things done. In other words, his ideas didn't take into account the basic universal laws that exist in the big pond. They were good ideas; don't get me wrong on that count. I've looked them over and I can tell you that not one of them was anything less than genius. But he was always bumping his head against management. Against the Big Pond. The place where he would never in a million years be allowed to swim. I tried to talk to him. I told him what I thought about his ideas. We knocked back many a Shiner Bock on that account. Him showing me a little drawing — done spur of the moment and showing me how the thing would be done in the real world — and me there just nodding and struck by the sheer brilliance and magnitude of it. But Brad was no Westinghouse. He didn't have the magnetic personality; he didn't have the credentials. I've read how George Westinghouse fronted a good deal of dough to a genius named Tesla over a few lines of telegraph type. You know, every one of those ideas is there for the world to read. They're all there in the U.S. Patent Office, just waiting for some future generation to look and see what could be done, if a fellow was smart enough to get what he was talking about. I swear to God, Tesla was a man hundreds of years before his time. Got some good books on him, you know. But Brad, Brad was maybe ten or twenty years before his time. Also, he didn't have the degree. Also, he wasn't a bona fide member of the Big Fish Club. And so he swam in small waters and raised hell. One day he raised too much. And now he's dead. All you have to do is talk to any one of his crew to verify what I'm telling you."

"Who was his crew?" I asked.

"Mainly Sandy Jones. Sandy is the token... uh, black guy. He lives first house just past the power plant. He's always the first one to work in the morning and the last one to leave each evening. Sandy, though — he's not the kind of fellow you could get a peep out of. I don't think he'll be much help. He's a parolee. Got a wife and four kids at home and works hard and never complains and keeps his family up."

"Okay," I said. "Why would CTL&P and Terry Throckmorton want to get rid of Brad Fisher?" And as I asked it, Throckmorton's name rang and reverberated in my head again. It was familiar, all right. I just couldn't place him.

Mike Fields looked down at the empty bottle of Shiner Bock in his hands. I could tell that he wanted more. I could also tell that he would rather not say what he was about to. But he said it, anyway. I found myself re-assessing the guy. Maybe Heidi knew him better. Maybe he was an overgrown kitten after all. And just maybe it took two Shiner Bocks tossed down quick and his wife riding herd on him to get him to admit anything.

"Because," he said, "Brad knew about the hole."

CHAPTER NINE

When Mike Fields said: "Brad knew about the hole," my cell phone rang.

It was Julie.

"Yeah, Babe?"

"Bill. I think..."

"What? What do you think? Is it —"

"Time? Yeah. Think so. Uh... contractions."

"I'm coming," I told her. "Call Penny and get her to take you to the hospital." Penny was my secretary. She had become, over the last few years, about as close as anyone could get without being family.

"I can drive, silly. I'm pregnant, not disabled. Besides," she said. "Penny is on a date."

"Yeah, but you're about to be a mom," I said. "And Penny can cancel her date."

"I'll drive," she told me, and the way she said it didn't allow room for argument.

"Okay. I'll be there inside two hours."

"Don't rush. I'll be fine."

We traded "*I love you*"s and hung up.

I told Mike and Heidi that my wife was about to have a baby. I tried to beat a hasty retreat.

Before heading out the door I turned back to the two of them.

"Mike, I'm going to be lead-footing it back to Austin. Can you at least make sure I won't get stopped on the way out of town?"

"I can do better than that," he said. "Hold on a minute."

Within five minutes it was all set. Not only was I not going to get stopped on the way out of town, but a state trooper was en-route to Mike's house to escort me all the way back to Austin.

The last thing Mike said to me — his cordless phone pressed hard into his ear as I started up my Mercedes — was: "Why didn't you tell me that your wife's uncle was the Lieutenant Governor?"

"Oh. You mean Nat Bierstone? He's just my partner. Besides, that's got nothing to do with anything."

"Bill. You don't need my help at all," Mike said.

"*Au contraire.* I need every bit of help I can get," I said, and I was off.

*****

The drive took an hour and ten minutes, but that was because we did ninety most of the way.

*****

"False alarm? What do you mean false alarm?"

The state trooper was chuckling. Shortly, I expected he'd be guffawing.

The nurse I was talking to kept a deadpan expression on her face.

"She's having contractions," I said. "How can it be a false alarm?"

"Mr. Travis. Voice down, please. Like I said, not false alarm. False *labor.*"

"Same thing," I said.

"Okay. Still, we want to keep her here overnight for observation."

"Observation, huh?" I was beginning to settle down a little. I'd been hopped up pretty much into overdrive ever since our brief phone conversation back in the Fields' tea garden.

"Yes. Observation. She rests. We monitor. That's about it."

"Is she in any danger? Will you have to, uh..."

"Induce labor? I don't think that's needed just yet. The doctor won't do that for at least another week."

I felt a gentle squeeze on my right elbow.

I looked. It was Julie's Uncle Nat.

"William. Julie will be fine. Let's go in and visit her."

"I'd like that," I said.

When I turned to look back, the state trooper was waving goodbye, headed toward the elevator.

Nat and I turned the corner, and before my hand even touched the door to Julie's room, there was explosive laughter from down the hall.

The things some people think are funny. I tell you.

CHAPTER TEN

It was late by the time I left St. David's Hospital. I'd spent an hour at Julie's side in her private room until I was thoroughly certain that she was getting enough of me being there and wanted me to leave. I told her I'd see her soon, kissed her and left.

Before I was out to my car I was on my cell phone. I called Mary Jo. I told her about Julie's false alarm. She informed me that she had company. Brad's little brother, Fred, had arrived and was fit to be tied. He was raising hell and had already called and threatened the Sheriff's Office, the County Coroner, and anybody else who would listen to him for more than a minute. He wanted his older brother's body and he wanted it right then.

All that was okay by me. Maybe it'd be him getting arrested instead of me. When Brad and I were kids we both thought that Freddie was a little demon, about like the kid on *The Omen.* Freddie could have been the Antichrist if he'd been a little quieter and had a dozen or so more points on his I.Q. score. I'd saved Brad's life once from the little brat. Freddie, who was about eight at the time, had picked up a pitchfork and was running full tilt at Brad's back with it, the needle-pointed silvery tines glinting in the sun. I took two steps, reached out and grasped the pitchfork. I wrenched it from Freddie's hands hard enough to give him splinters.

No. I didn't mind if Freddie raised hell.

As I was listening to Mary Jo and getting into my car in the hospital parking garage, I remembered something that Mike Fields had said.

Something about Brad explaining his drawings to Mike over a few beers. I'd have to see those drawings. Also I wanted to talk to — what was his name? Jones? Yeah. Jones. Token black guy, as Mike had put it. Wife and four kids at home.

I told Mary Jo I was on my way back to town but that I'd get a hotel room. She tried to get me to commit to staying at her home, but there was no way that was going to happen. I wouldn't be sleeping under the same roof with Freddie during this lifetime, and knowing Freddie, he'd be sleeping on the living room couch, the only place to sleep in the whole house other than Mary Jo's bedroom.

By the time I was in my car and pulling back onto the highway headed back to Bryan and College Station, I was beginning to get a glimmer of just who the hell Terry Throckmorton was as the advancing little world encompassed by my headlights moved across the Texas miles.

*****

What in hell was "The Hole?" It was the big and dark question that filled my thoughts as I returned to the outskirts of Bryan, Texas. The question had been gnawing away at the far back corners of my mind during the entire return trip.

I'd have to find out, and pretty quick.

I checked in at an older hotel I remembered, built during the 60s and built to last. I had never been a Marriott or a Hilton type of guy. And while the twin cities had both famous hotels, I was looking for some-thing a little more homey and familiar. So I got an interior room up on the second floor with my window overlooking what used to be a Kettle Restaurant but that was now some Tex-Mex joint.

Before getting to sleep I called Julie. Yeah, I'd woken her up. She was fine. No. No contractions. No more false labor, she corrected me, as opposed to false alarms.

We exchanged an "I love you" again, and said goodnight.

It took until nearly 1:00 a.m. for me to get to sleep. And, of course, I had a nightmare. But then, don't I always?

The coming darkness took me down, down into an abyss the like of which I had never before encountered. The abyss was where I could talk with Brad and finally get some answers.

I was surprised to find it was no more than a hole. A very deep hole.

"I don't know, Bill," Brad said. "You're going off half-cocked again."

Brad had a shovel in his hand, and he was shoveling something black and raw and awfully smelly into a furnace.

"Why?" I asked. "All I want to know is what happened? And who?"

"Yeah. That's just like you, Bill. You never could leave well enough alone."

"It's smelly down here," I said.

"It's all this dragon poop," he said. "Makes good fuel, though."

"I'm sure. We used to shovel stuff just like this."

"That's right. I remember now."

He stopped shoveling and stood with his arms across the handle for support.

"Bill," he said. "I'm dead."

"I know, Brad. I'm sorry. You should have talked to me."

"It wouldn't have helped. Somebody had to fall."

"Why?"

"Why? Why. Always why. Some things just are," he said. "Leave me alone for awhile, will you? I'm dead. We're not supposed to be talking. Company policy."

"Sorry," I said. "Goodbye, Brad."

But Brad never said another word.

*****

I awoke at ten till nine with a slightly stuffy head, red eyes and the hunger of a she-wolf with a litter of pups.

By ten twenty I found a good diner that served up a decent breakfast.

At a little after eleven, I was back at Mary Jo's.

CHAPTER ELEVEN

Mike and I were under the live oak tree a dozen yards from Mary Jo's kitchen door. Each of us had a beer in hand. Mary Jo was in the kitchen cutting up chicken. I figured we'd smell it frying soon.

There with us was Freddie Fisher. The beer was strictly off-limits for him. Mary Jo had alluded to his heart condition. There I was, about to turn forty-one, and here was this kid with something wrong with his heart. Go figure. Then again, I've known habitually angry people, and if chronic anger isn't a risk factor for heart disease then there isn't such a thing.

Mike continued his story from the previous evening, and the two of us listened, me sipping a beer, and Freddie drinking tepid water. Life was sometimes kind.

In 1990 my friend Bradley took a summer temporary job at the Navasota Lignite Plant #2 seventeen miles east of College Station, Texas, just across the Navasota River in Grimes County. His chief duty was to do what he was told, and during that hottest of summers he kept his hands wrapped around a long-nosed shovel and spent his days covering a fuel pipe that was being laid from the plant to the lignite strip-mine coal fields.

After the pipe was laid the crew was paid off and dismissed, all but Brad, who complained little and was ever eager to get his hands dirty.

Mike didn't believe that Brad learned about The Hole until sometime the next spring, and by that time he was full-time and busy completing endless rounds of safety-inspections. When anything got red-tagged — and there were a lot of red-tags flying around in those days before government de-regulation — Brad's job was to fix it. By that time he was certified as an electrician by the State, having spent his off hours during the week nights in class over at the Texas A&M Riverside Campus.

"When he found out about The Hole," Mike said, "he did what every new boot did. He asked questions. I wasn't his supervisor then, so I don't know for sure what he was told, and we only had the one conversation about it."

"When?" I asked.

"Two weeks ago."

"Tell me about the hole, Mike."

"There's no telling how many of them there are spread around the continental United States, in forests, deserts, near small communities. One of these days, say ten thousand years from now, whatever passes for human will stumble across the one we have at CTL&P. And bad things will start happening. That's if the technology of the time is sufficiently low. If it's high, no doubt the people of that later time will clean it all up. Maybe they'll disintegrate everything, you know, like *Star Wars* or something. Or they'll fire it all off into the sun. But until that day, The Hole and its contents will be there. You couldn't get me near the damn thing.

"Forget seeing it yourself. Last thing I heard it was sealed off. And good riddance.

"Okay. Think of all the limestone caves there are underneath Texas. That's where our groundwater comes from. The rain comes down, permeates through the soil, gets filtered through a thick layer of limestone formation, and runs off into underground rivers, what we call aquifers. The cleanest water on earth. But water does strange things. I'm no geologist, but from what little I've read about it, the water carves out weak places in the limestone, cuts channels through the chalk, and what's left are endless miles of caverns down there in the dark. Some are solitary, cut off from others. Some run in chains, with narrow, snaking passages between them. A good spelunker could go down there and spend a lifetime looking, and never explore a thousandth of the entire labyrinth. Some are fairly close to the surface, and every once in a while somebody breaks through and discovers one. You've got the Natural Bridge Caverns over in New Braunfels, and the Wonder Cave in San Marcos. Out west there are the Caverns of Sonora. Just north of Austin, near Georgetown, highway workers discovered the Inner Space Caves while taking core samples during the construction of Interstate 35. So, it was only natural that a strip mining company would discover what we call The Hole during the early 1990s.

"After a few employee deaths during early exploration, it became sort of company policy to keep it under our hats.

"But then along came Terry Throckmorton, at that time a junior member of the Board of Directors. Instead of a hole in the earth that swallowed people, he saw dollar signs.

"And that's when the core rods started coming in.

*****

When Mike said the name "Terry Throckmorton", I got another one of those long chills that physically shook me. I don't think he noticed, as it was his fourth or fifth beer. Who was counting? I wasn't. I was sipping my third. I think.

Mike Fields was done talking. The three of us trundled back into the house, compelled by the growing dark and the over-powering smell of chicken frying. I was hungry. Also, I wanted Mary Jo's company, her smile and her gentle nature.

We all sat down at the kitchen table and ate. About halfway through dinner, when there was only the sound of forks on plates and men gobbling good home-cooked food, Mary Jo broke down into a fit of crying. Freddie tried his hand at consoling her — which was one of the oddest quirks of human nature I believe I've ever witnessed — but she wasn't having any of it. She got up and headed for her bedroom and shut the door. I heard the latch click into place.

Mike Fields just kept looking down at his plate. From that I gathered he was the kind of guy who couldn't handle emotional outbursts or awkward social situations. I'd begun to feel a grudging respect for the man, and I felt a little embarrassed for him.

When we finished dinner I got up and washed my dish and my glass and put them in the dish drain. I went back to Mary Jo's door.

"Mary Jo," I said quietly, and tapped on her door with a knuckle.

"Bill?"

"Yeah. We gotta go, Hon," I told her.

"Where?"

"To see Brad," I told her. "Bring your jacket."

CHAPTER TWELVE

While there may be a governmental entity locally referred to as the coroner's office, in practice it was little more than a sterile, cold, and badly lit room in the bowels of a local hospital.

It was just the two of us. I understood Mike Fields' demurral to come with us, but still, I would have felt a little better about going in with the big man at my back.

"You're sure you want to do this?" I asked Mary Jo. I knew I didn't. The picture I had conjured in my head was bad enough, thanks to enough movies by George Romero and Stephen Spielberg.

"I'll be fine, Bill," she said. A good liar, that Mary Jo.

A young fellow, no more than about twenty-eight and wearing garish green and orange scrubs, got up from a desk across the cold room and walked towards us.

"Can I help you?" he asked.

"This is Mary Jo Fisher. Her husband is Brad Fisher. Was, that is. She's here to see the body."

"Sure," he said. "Come on." He wore a relaxed attitude and a jovial smirk like he wore his scrubs — too much and out-of-place.

"Thank you," Mary Jo said.

We followed him to a bank of drawers and without checking to make sure it was the right one, he pulled on a handle low to the floor.

*****

Brad's body bore not so much as a mark. He could have been merely asleep, had it not been for his bluish and steely-gray pallor.

Beside me I heard Mary Jo's sharp intake of breath.

"Mary Jo?" I asked.

"Why is he dead, Bill? He looks fine."

"Mary Jo," I said. "Mary Jo. This is just the husk. Brad's gone. I don't know why."

It happened then. The floodgates opened. The dam burst. She was on her knees, her body thrown across his.

I could make out only a few words of what she said between the wracking sobs: "Cold. So cold... my Brad."

I looked at the intern — doctor, whatever the hell he was. He rolled his eyes at the ceiling, and then met my gaze.

I frowned at him. It was so much nicer than putting his lights out, at least for him.

"You got a report?" I asked him. "Any kind of report?"

"Yeah," he said. "There was no autopsy. Just the coroner's report."

"Why's that?" I asked.

"He had all the outward signs of high voltage. You know, frizzed hair, muscular contraction. This guy was jolted."

"Fine," I said. "Let me see a copy."

I noticed he was distracted by Mary Jo's hovering over Brad's body. She stroked his brow with her fingertips and whispered something to him.

"Sure," he said, finally, then: "Can you make her stop that?"

I gave him a hard stare for a moment, and he got the communication. He held up his hands: *fine, sorry.*

I knelt beside Mary Jo.

"Mary Jo," I whispered. "Time to go." But my eyes were on Brad's face.

Old friend, I thought, *why didn't you call me? Why didn't you let her call me?*

Brad said not a word, and I suppose that was fitting. He rarely had in life.

"Mary Jo?" I pressed, gently.

"Okay, Bill. I'll be all right," she said, quietly.

"I know."

I helped her to her feet. She opened her small purse, removed a tiny flower and placed it on his bare chest. The bud of a passion flower. I wondered what the next person along to open Brad's drawer would think. To hell with it.

I reached down and pushed gently on the drawer, and Brad rolled slowly back into the darkness.

"Goodbye," I whispered to him.

"Let's get the fuck out of here, Bill," Mary Jo whispered to me.

*****

We left the hospital, two page report in hand, and wandered out into the parking lot. Overhead thick clouds were rolling in, piling up on top of each other. I could smell the rain before the first drop fell.

CHAPTER THIRTEEN

Core rods, Mike had said.

The words moved around inside my head like a steel ball in a pinball machine.

"Where are we going, Bill?" Mary Jo asked. "This isn't the way home."

"To see somebody," I said.

The traffic was nervous with the anticipation of the impending downpour. A couple of thick drops thocked against my windshield.

"Who?"

"One of the guys Brad worked with. The token black guy."

"That would be Jones," she said. "You know where he lives?"

"Sort of. You got a first name?"

"Irvin, I think. Something like that. Although I think he goes by some nickname." Mary Jo took a look around her at where we were going. "We going to the plant?"

"I hope not, but maybe. Today's a Wednesday. He could be at work, but it's after hours. Unless, that is, he works second shift."

"Do you believe in ghosts, Bill?" she asked as I pulled in behind a large concrete truck at the next red light. We'd be turning due east for awhile, then south.

"Why do you ask?"

"Because..."

"Spit it out, Mary Jo," I said.

"Because every since Brad died, I've been feeling like I'm being watched. Just... every moment. That's all."

There was silence in the car for a moment. I was expecting her to ask me if I had a sense that Brad was hanging out close by, checking things out. Instead Mary Jo lapsed into silence.

"Okay," I said.

*****

The rain came down in sheets.

Along the highway a mile past the power plant entrance, there was a row of dingy houses. These were working people, I could tell right off. Through the rain I could make out old pickup trucks that had seen better days, rusted A-frames for hoisting engine blocks, blue tarpaulins covering God knows what-all, and cast-off toys everywhere.

I pulled into the first driveway.

"Wait here, Mary Jo," I said. And stay dry."

I reached under my seat for my umbrella, and not finding it realized that I had left it at my office. Great.

"You're gonna get soaked, Bill," she said when I came away with nothing.

"Yeah. Be right back."

I was on the front porch within a few seconds, but in that brief space I managed to get completely drenched. Water squished in my shoes.

The doorbell hung from the wall on twisted wire. It looked dead.

I knocked.

The front door opened and I heard the babble of children's voices in the background and a loud television — cartoons. I could smell boiling cabbage.

"Yes?" the woman asked.

She was very pretty but her face was implacably bored — a mid-thirty-ish looker with a light movie star complexion; she was the mother of all those voices inside.

"I'm looking for the Jones family. Do they live close by?"

"Who wants to know?"

I didn't have to think about it. People are usually able to spot a lie from a mile away, and truth is usually best, if uncomfortable.

"Ma'am, my name is Bill Travis. I'm looking for the Mr. Jones who works at the power plant. His foreman, Brad Fisher, was killed, and I was Brad's best friend."

I waited.

She looked past me, out into the rain, then fixed her eyes on me, appraising.

"Come in. I'm Dorothy Jones. My husband is home sick today." She pushed on the screen door.

I turned toward the car and tried to give Mary Jo the thumbs up, but I doubted she could see me through the pouring rain.

The house was clean but for the toys scattered everywhere. On the couch there was a bored teen-aged boy of about fourteen, and on the floor three kids dismissed me with a glance and returned to watching some strange Japanese anime cartoon I'd never seen before.

"Come on back to the kitchen, Mr. Travis," Dorothy Jones said. "You can't hear yourself think in here."

"Sandy!" Dorothy called out from the hallway to the kitchen, toward the rear of the house.

"What?"

"You got company."

"I'm sick, Dotty."

"You're not too sick to sit and talk," she replied.

The kitchen was clean. On the stove there was a pot of black-eyed peas just starting to boil over and the cabbage pot with its lid starting to do a little dance.

"Damn," Dotty said. "Have a seat, Mr. Travis. Sandy's gotta get his shirt on. You can't leave food cooking for two minutes."

"Fine," I said.

"Iced tea?" she asked.

"Yes ma'am."

Dotty Jones turned the fire down low on the peas, shifted the lid on the cabbage to let the steam blow off, and turned to the refrigerator and opened it.

"You're soaked, Bill Travis," she said.

"Yes ma'am."

"I'll get you a towel."

She poured a glass of tea and set it before me and walked out of the kitchen to return with a clean towel.

"You coming, Sandy?" she called out loudly.

"I'm coming. I'm coming," the voice was tired, hoarse, and resigned, all at once.

She draped the towel over my shoulders and I used it to wipe my face.

"Thanks," I said.

"Fiddlesticks," she said.

Sandy Jones emerged into the kitchen, buttoning the last two buttons of his shirt as he came. He was a tall man with a bit of graying grizzle in his sideburns.

I started to stand, but he held up a long-fingered hand.

"Keep your seat, stranger. We don't stand on ceremony around here. You selling life insurance?"

I laughed. "It would be easier if I was," I said.

"What are you selling, then?"

"He ain't selling nothing," Dorothy Jones said. "This is Bill Travis, Brad Fisher's best friend."

I watched his face as she said it, and it sagged all of an inch.

"What you want?" he asked me.

"Sit down, Sandy," Dotty said. "Be kind. His best friend just died."

Sandy Jones sat down across from me.

"You're wet," he said.

"Yeah." I did the best I could with the towel and launched into the questions before Sandy Jones had a chance to think of what he was going to say.

"Can you tell me about core rods and the hole and how Brad Fisher died? And why?"

"Shit," he said. "Just like that?"

"Just like that," I said.

"Look Mister..."

"Bill," I said, maintaining a thin smile.

"Bill. Fine. Look... I've got a family to look after. I have to report to a parole officer once a week who doesn't give a shit about me or my family. I can't get caught up in anything."

"Sure," I said. "If you are able, I'd like to know those three things, and then I'll disappear back into the rain."

"Tell him, Sandy," his wife said, hot pot of steaming cabbage in hand. "You can't even sleep right. You've got to tell somebody. This fellow is your chance."

"He ain't my chance if I lose my job."

"If you lose that damned job I'll dance with bells on my toes. You're a hard worker. There's always a job for you, and maybe a job where somebody will appreciate you."

Sandy Jones signed, loudly.

And then he told me.

*****

"Them things are scattered all over the place, and they'll kill you if you get too close or stay too long. Core rods, you know. It's the radiation. I was there when the first ones came through and I've seen the trucks come and go. I even know the name of the driver. They're in the hole, deep down there. They have them placed in bundles of no more than five at a time. I think one of them is enough to kill a man. One is dangerous. Five? Don't get me started. I've done some thinking on it. What can they do with those old rods that come from the nuke plants? It's about money, that's all. And the hole is just a little cave that leads down to a big cavern. There's a whole series of those caverns. I spent a whole weekend down there one time, and found some stuff that shouldn't have been there."

"What kind of stuff, Sandy?" I asked.

"A lot of Indian pottery, arrowheads and stuff. Skeletons too. Then there's the chests and the diary."

"What diary?"

"It's in French. I don't know French."

"You got it here?"

"Yeah. I'll show it to you. Mr. Travis, you believe in ghosts?"

I shivered, and not from my dampened condition. It was the second time that day I'd heard that question.

"Why?" I asked.

"You wouldn't believe me if I told you."

"Try me, Sandy."

"'Cause one of those chests is haunted."

CHAPTER FOURTEEN

I tried to piece together as much of the journal as I could, there in Sandy and Dorothy Jones' living room. The book was written in several hands, beginning with the original owner, Louis du Orly. That name I could make out, but little of the remainder of it. My French was not good.

I handed the journal back to Sandy Jones and got up and stretched my legs. I nodded to Dorothy Jones and headed for the front door.

"Mr. Travis," Sandy said. "Maybe you should hold onto this. I've got no real use for it." He handed the journal back to me.

We stepped outside.

"Well, if it's all right with you," I said. "How about I make a copy of it and return the original to you?"

The rain had slackened to a drizzle once again.

"That's fine. Whatever. Mr. Travis, I think you should see that hole."

"Call me Bill," I said. "I do want to see that hole. But I've got a woman in the car who needs to get home. I'm not sure of her safety at this point."

"Safest place for her would be here with my wife," he said, and I met his searching gaze.

It felt right. There were things going on that I had no idea about. And I still hadn't seen that investigator that Mary Jo had told me about. Mike Fields was probably on the job just now at the power plant up the road. I was unsure how safe Mary Jo would be at home without me around. Not until a few things were settled.

"Sandy," I said. "How safe is that hole? What I mean is, I've got a wife of my own at home with a baby coming, and she'll be mad as hell if I come home in a pine box.

"I know where all the booby traps are, Bill," he said.

I looked toward the car. Mary Jo yawned, caught sight of me, then gave a little bored wave.

"When do you want to do this?" I asked him.

"It's right now or not at all," he said.

"Why 'not at all'?"

"Because, I'm supposed to be home sick. I've got to work tomorrow. After that, the only chance is the weekend, and that place is closed off tighter than a four by four shoved up a cow's ass."

"That's pretty tight, Sandy," I said.

*****

Mary Jo was delighted at the prospect of staying with Dotty Jones and her kids while Sandy was to "show me a few things."

"You two be careful," Dotty Jones called out through the screen door as we stepped into the drizzle.

I turned back to her. "Mrs. Jones. I'm never careful. What I am, though, is thorough."

"Good enough," she said.

I stopped by my car, placed the journal, all wrapped up as it was with cellophane, under the driver's seat and out of sight. I locked the car all the way around and then followed Sandy to his battered Ford pickup and climbed inside.

"That woman," he said, depositing a pretty beat-up five gallon brown paper sack filled with flashlights and other odds and ends on the floorboard at my feet. The old truck smelled like spent cigarette butts and old sweat.

"Who?" I asked.

"My wife. She's good," he said, "don't get me wrong, but she thinks too much."

"I don't know," I replied. "I like a woman who thinks for herself."

"Got one of those, do you?"

"Damn right," I said.

"She trouble?"

"Plenty."

"Good," he said, and turned the ignition key. "I hate bein' wrong. She pretty?"

"Yeah," I said.

"Even better."

*****

Instead of going to the power plant main gate, Sandy turned off to the left several hundred yards to the south of it, got out and fished out a key for the large pad lock on the single bar steel gate, pulled through, then went back and locked it up again.

"The lock was on," he said, once back inside the truck, "which usually means that no one is around. But just in case, if anybody sees us, you're an inspector from the state office."

"You mean lie about it? I don't have any kind of a badge to convince anybody."

"So. Just act like a jerk and stare them down. That usually works, because these people can't think for themselves. They've got to have somebody higher up do their thinking for them."

"Okay," I said.

We bounced along a muddied, caliche-gravel path through stands of trees and across an open field. Cows stopped chewing on wet grass and stared at us.

"All of this was strip-mined a few years back," Sandy moved his hand to take in the whole field. "Lignite field, you know. Had to put it all back the way they found it, or mostly, and it's starting to grow back a little now."

I nodded.

We went over a hill and down a winding course that threaded close to the trees again.

"It was found during the lignite years, early on."

"Who found it?" I asked.

"Me," Sandy said.

"Oh."

"I thought about not reporting it, but then somebody else would have fallen in and gotten themselves killed, and I didn't want anything like that bothering me, you know?"

"Yeah."

After ten minutes of driving through the rough countryside, Sandy pulled off the narrow gravel path and behind a stand of yaupon scrub and stopped.

"We walk from here," he said. "I don't want my truck tracks anywhere near it."

"Fine," I said.

We got out. The clouds overhead were dispersing and to the west the sun was trying to poke through.

"Good timing," Sandy said. "I didn't want to get too wet."

We walked, cutting through the scrub brush along what could be described as no more than a cow path. My shoes picked up a good deal of mud, but I scraped it off whenever I could; here on a mat of thick weeds, there on a fallen tree branch.

After ten minutes we came around yet another stand of brush behind a high board fence that looked as out of place in a cow pasture as my Dr. Martens shoes.

Behind the fence I could make out a tin roof.

"It's supposed to look like a barn, but it doesn't have much floor on the inside of it, if you know what I mean."

Sandy rounded the fence and I followed. We came to yet another padlock that resembled the first and Sandy used a key from his large key ring, opened the lock and we slipped through.

The wooden building was nestled inside the fence with no more than a few feet between them. The door in front of us had a simple board with a single nail through it into the front wall which Sandy turned easily. The door opened.

Sandy reached in the bag, clicked on his flashlight and inspected the interior.

"Anybody home?" he called out. I heard a dim echo. Sandy laughed.

"Nope," he said. "Just us chickens."

He reached up and tugged on a string and an electric light came on.

*****

The hole was twelve feet wide by about ten long, and encompassed half the interior floor space.

The smell was musty and strong.

"Smells like mold and chlorine," I said, then I pegged it. "Bats, I'll bet."

"Hell, yes," Sandy said. "Used to be millions of 'em, but we killed most of 'em."

"Another environmental catastrophe," I said.

"That's what I thought, too. Ever' time I have to slap a mosquito, I think about all those dead bats."

From the electric bulb overhead and Sandy's wandering flashlight I could make out the rough, dry walls of the hole. Ten feet down the topsoil gave out and what appeared to be shale and rock took its place.

"Over here," Sandy said.

I looked where his light flicked and there was a steel boom against a side wall with a basket configuration and a motor and winch.

"That doesn't look promising," I said.

"Oh, it's safe. If it can hold Mike Fields, it can hold you and me."

"That's what I was afraid of," I said.

Sandy laughed again, and I couldn't help smiling.

*****

"Stupid question," I said, fifty feet below the surface. Above, the dwindling light looked a world away, and below, only blackness. Sandy had one hand around the steel cable and the other around the flashlight.

"What?" he asked, and shined his light on the walls.

"How do we get back up?"

"Damn, forgot about that!" he said.

"What?"

"Just kidding. Look, all we have to do is give the line a jerk to make sure it's tight, then hit a switch down there that reverses the winch."

"Oh."

Down, down into the darkness. The air grew cooler and more dank.

The floor came up to meet us, or at least it felt that way, and I removed the safety rope and clip from the cable.

"How far down are we?" I asked, and my voice traveled long and far and came back to me in a faint echo.

"Couple of hundred feet."

"Just asking," I said.

Sandy handed me a flashlight

I clicked my light on, panned it about. The hole above us had tapered until it was a very narrow entrance to the small cavern where we stood. To my left was another narrow entryway to a larger, darker space beyond.

"Not that way," Sandy said.

"Core rods?" I asked.

"You betcha. Come on," he said.

*****

Sandy led me through an even narrower passage that opened out after a dozen yards into a large cavern that swallowed our light.

I felt a drop of water on the top of my head.

"It's raining," I said.

"You're no spelunker, Bill Travis."

"I know."

"Stalactites dripping is what that is. Always dripping, especially after a hard rain."

I followed Sandy along a limestone trail. The place was awash with little sparkles of light reflecting back from our flashlight beams. Great stalagmites grew from the cavern floor like the boles of bald cypress. Pools of translucent and milky water were everywhere.

"Watch your step, Bill," Sandy said.

"Sure thing."

"It's the next cavern over."

"The chests?"

"Yeah."

I followed him along the undulating path, the rough, hard floor of the cavern dipping down toward little pools of water, then abruptly up again over small ridges. I would have to do some studying up on caves and cave systems.

We went through another narrow crevice and we had to turn sideways, duck down and slink our way through.

The cavern we emerged into was decidedly different from the first. Here the stalagmites were larger, some meeting their mates a third of the way up to form great columns. How long would that take? I did know that they formed slowly, over hundreds and even thousands of years drip by infinitesimal drip. How much building matter could be contained in one drop of water? A few thousand molecules? Who knew? All I did know was that the cavern was old. Older than man? Perhaps. Was it here when dinosaurs roamed the Earth? Probably not.

"Look, Bill," Sandy said.

I turned my light to follow his, and there, high up on the cavern wall was a treasure beyond price.

We were looking at a pictograph mural of vast extent, etched into the wall. It began six feet up and went as high as thirty feet. I began to imagine the amount of labor the endeavor had required, and all of it high work. Where were the pole marks against the walls? An image leapt into my head of a tower of natives standing on the shoulders of the one below him until there was a neat ladder of six or seven of them. God! Who knew how it was done?

"Indians," I said. "But which tribe?"

"I don't know anything about it," Sandy said. "Maybe many different tribes over lots of years. It just... it feels old."

"Yeah."

We went along the wall slowly, moving our lights between it and the floor so as to assure our footing.

There were symbols there that I had seen in textbooks, and many others I'd never seen, perhaps no one in modern times had seen. The sun and moon were prominent, not in size, but in recognizability and repetition. Warriors with spears and bows, tepees, pregnant maidens, bison herds, strange floating icons which were likely weather phenomena or shooting stars. A wooly mammoth being brought down with shillelaghs! I picked out a comet. And then came the oddest and creepiest of all: a sailing ship, complete with square-rigged sails and ropes and a bow effigy of a woman with large breasts.

"Damn," I said.

"Yeah. Bill, we can't stay here long. There's a stack of core rods over there. No one knows how radioactive they are, so it's better we keep moving."

I swung my flashlight in the direction he indicated, and thirty feet away on the floor of the cavern was a dingy metal rack with five steel tubes.

"Jesus," I said.

"Come on. We're almost there."

*****

"It's gone," Sandy said. He stood on a hump of limestone and shined his light into a large alcove.

"Thieves," I said. "Desecrators."

"Desecrators," Sandy repeated. "That's a big word. Sounds pretty bad."

"It is. It's anybody that robs a tomb or destroys something of benefit to mankind. How many chests were there?"

"Five big ones and one small one."

"The small one..." I began.

"Yeah. The one that was haunted," he said.

Sandy shined his light along the floor close by.

"Check this out," he said. I saw what he meant. There were grooves in the cavern floor, going back the way we'd come.

"Tell me what you think," I said.

"I didn't think anybody knew about the crates except me."

"Did you ever open them?"

He hesitated.

"You'd better spill it," I said.

"Okay," he signed. "I did open one."

"The haunted one?"

"No. I wouldn't have touched that one for anything. No. One of the others."

"And you took something," I said, matter-of-factly.

"Yeah."

"What'd you find, and what'd you take?"

"A croker sack full of gold, rubies, and big green gems."

"What about the skeletons?" I asked. "You said somcthing before about skeletons."

"Oh. Oh shit. You're right."

"What?"

"They're gone."

CHAPTER FIFTEEN

It was growing dark by the time we made it back to Sandy and Dotty Jones' place. A full moon was on the rise, its white, skeletal glow spectral between a branchwork of dark oak and other, unnamable trees.

Inside, the television was silent. Mary Jo, Dotty and three kids sat around the living room coffee table playing Monopoly.

"Who's winning?" I asked.

Mary Jo looked up as we tromped in.

"Bill!" she said. "You looked like you fell in a hole somewhere."

"Practically," I said.

Dotty and Sandy exchanged knowing looks.

"Sorry to interrupt your game," I said, "but I think it's time I took you home, Mary Jo."

"Nonsense. I'm winning."

And so she was. There was a stack of bills in front of her nearly an inch high while all the other players were dealing with singleton ones, fives, twenties and fifties. Most of Mary Jo's bills were yellow and orange.

"Looks like it," I said.

Sandy and I stood there over their shoulders and watched. It was all over but the shouting. One kid, Ames, the littlest, went around the board three times dodging all of Mary Jo's hotels and paying out most of the two hundred he collected each time to the pile in the middle of the board. He was stuck in jail and about to roll the dice again when there was a resounding double thump at the front door.

I felt a chill.

If that was friendly knock, then I had never heard one.

The house was suddenly quiet. Not a movement, not a peep came from the table. Mary Jo's eyes met mine. They were eyes of fear.

"Open up, goddammit!" someone outside shouted.

Sandy was moving toward the door on the balls of his feet. I grasped his elbow and shook my head "no" silently when he turned to look back at me.

"Let me," I whispered.

I moved behind the front door. I reached over and turned the lock very slowly, hoping it couldn't be heard outside.

The man outside cursed, as if to himself, although I wasn't ready to rule out that he had someone with him. Then I heard it: "Goddamned niggers."

I mouthed to Sandy: "You got a gun?"

It was a stupid question, I thought. Sandy was a felon, on parole. He would never be allowed to own a gun again in his life.

"Yes," he nodded.

He reached behind the chair in the corner and brought out a twelve gauge shotgun. I watched as he thumbed the safety off.

I mouthed to Dotty: "Back door. Lock it."

I'd almost told her to call the sheriff's office, but then I remembered that Sandy was a felon. The sheriff was the last person we needed to call.

The front door shook in its facing to a hard rap from outside and I nearly leapt out of my skin.

"Open up!" the man at the door shouted. "Or I'm coming inside."

From five feet away and almost a forty-five degree angle, Sandy held the scattergun pointed at the center of the front door.

"Hey out there!" I raised my voice. "Anybody coming in is coming in dead!"

I listened close beside the door. There were whispers and a squish of shoes going around the corner of the house out there. They were circling around. Then I heard it. A loud sigh, not three feet from me on the other side of the door. There was more than one of them.

"Look" the gruff voice said. "I'm going to make this easy. Tell that nigger in there to throw out that sack of gold and shit, or we'll burn your asses out of there."

I looked over at Mary Jo. She was trying to say something, but I couldn't make out what she was mouthing at me.

"Get those kids down on the floor," I hissed at her, as quietly as I could, but so that I knew she would hear me.

Sandy took two steps to the front door, coming perfectly in line with it.

I looked at him standing there, casting his tall shadow on the front door from the lamp behind him. He was shaking, but not with fear.

"Nobody," he said quietly, "is going to threaten my family."

"Sandy," I said, "don't."

But he did.

The roar was that of lightning splitting a tree, and it reverberated inside the house and in my head for a good long time to come.

*****

Before opening the front door I reached over and plucked the shotgun from Sandy's hand. I peeked outside.

There was a horrible jagged hole in the center of the Jones' front door, and outside, at the foot of the steps, I saw another jagged hole in the chest of the man who had been standing there.

His breathing was ragged and there was a perplexity on his face. Several feet away there was a large silvery handgun glinting in the porch light. I suddenly knew it was what he'd rapped the front door with.

I turned to Sandy.

"This is *my* shotgun, Sandy," I said. "It was *always* my gun. I came to ask you if you would take me coon hunting and I brought my own gun, got it?"

He stood there, in shock. In the front yard the wounded man was moaning, if not dying.

"You're a felon. You see a parole officer once a week. Remember? It's my gun, got it?" I asked again.

"Okay," he said.

"Good. There's another one out there. I'm going out there. You're staying in here. Close this door and lock it. And call the Sheriff."

"Thank you, Bill," he said.

I glanced back at the children, who were looking at their father's back and then at me. A knowingness passed between us, all of us.

"Thank you, Mr. Bill," the oldest boy said.

Dotty was standing there behind the table, her hands pressed against her mouth.

"Take care of them, Mary Jo," I said, then turned to face the open doorway and the dying man beyond.

"Lock it behind me, Sandy," I said, and went out into the night.

For any man or woman there is a fluidity to things that takes hold whenever action is required and thought and reason must be thrust aside. The air takes on a crispness as it surges into the lungs. The thrum of the heart beats a drum-like pace against the inner ear. The throat constricts and becomes an arid yet slippery ditch that words cannot climb out of. There is only intention, and the being is salved by the purity of it. It is more powerful, more real than any drug-induced state could hope to emulate, and in the final analysis it is euphoric — so euphoric it hurts. That's what I felt as I stepped down from Sandy Jones' front porch.

So many things came into me at once and in an instant I sorted them all and placed them all in their proper repositories, tagging each by relative importance: the extra truck and car parked on the side of the highway closer to Sandy Jones' house than to his next door neighbor; the wetness of the porch and the muddied tracks there, both mine and Sandy's and the dying man's; the swish of someone running through high grass from the rear of the house; the neighbor's front porch light coming on; a car passing by on the highway, it's high-beams flicking off as another car hove into view around the corner; the moisture in the air; names winnowing up to the surface of a pond inside my head; and finally my own feet and hands, moving as if of their own accord.

I raised the shotgun as a figure emerged from the blackness beside the house at a dead run.

"Hold it!" the words leapt from my throat, unbidden.

The shotgun in my hands tracked him even as he came to a slip-sliding stop and a hand waved in the air, a gun subtended from it for balance at the last moment.

"Drop it!" I yelled.

"Dad?!" The young man said. His attention wasn't on me, but instead on the large man at my feet.

"Drop it!" I said softly.

His arms came down, lax. He still held the gun. I wasn't sure whether or not he knew he had one there. I wanted it gone before he realized it.

I took five quick steps toward him and jerked it out of his hand and threw it into the shadow.

"Daddy?" he said to the man on the ground.

"I'm sorry, son," I said.

"Daddy?"

"Go to him," I said.

The kid went. He was no more than a high school kid, perhaps seventeen.

He knelt down into the wet grass and mud and lifted the man's head.

I came close to them, hovering, hovering. I could have been a hummingbird, I felt so small and out of place. How suddenly everything can change.

There was blood on the man's lips. The kid tried to wipe it away, but more came.

"Call an ambulance," I turned and yelled at the neighbor on his front porch.

"There's... no need," the man said, and coughed.

"Why, Daddy?" the kid cried.

"I'm killed, son," he said, and those were his last words.

CHAPTER SIXTEEN

I'd forgotten. The Jones' house was across the county line into Grimes County. I remembered the instant the first of several sheriff's cruisers pulled up to the house.

An ambulance came and then turned around and went back when it was discovered their patient was deceased. We waited for the coroner, and while we waited, the house had more men and women in it in uniform than I had ever seen inside a police station at once.

A blue plastic tarpaulin covered the body outside. The kid was standing there, dazed. Sheriff's deputies tried talking to him. He had handcuffs on, but if he came fully awake and aware, I was ready. He'd been coming for me, which was a little odd, seeing as how I had on handcuffs as well.

Dotty and the kids were at the neighbor's house, and occasionally one came outside onto the front porch, but a slender black hand quickly came out and hauled him or her back inside. Eventually the neighbor's front porch light clicked off. I was thankful. I didn't want anyone of the present crew going over there.

"Why'd you shoot him, Mr. Travis?" a man asked me for the dozenth time, hoping I would change my story. When I didn't answer him he said: "Are you sure somebody else didn't shoot him?"

I didn't answer. I was watching the kid, who didn't seem to know I was even there. It was likely he'd be figuring it out before long. He'd remember me, and it would come in a roaring flood back to him, and then there would be hell to pay.

"It would be easier if you cooperated with us, Mr. Travis," another deputy said.

"Call me Bill," I said. It was my grandest admission that night.

Sandy Jones was being questioned separately by five deputies at once. They were poking him and prodding him with words. I was hoping he wouldn't spring the wrong leak.

We watched as the body was carefully photographed, the flashes like localized lightning, before it was loaded into the coroner's wagon, which took over an hour to arrive from Anderson, the county seat. The boy was packed into the rear of a sheriff's vehicle, a sheriff's deputy's hand on his head pushing downward so he wouldn't bump it going in.

Five minutes later someone found the other pistol. I was hoping my prints weren't on it. That would take even further explaining. As I recalled it hadn't been in my hand but a second before it went flying into the wet grass and the darkness.

An hour later the cuffs were removed from my wrists.

I stood and waited.

The sheriff had finally arrived and I was about to get a lecture.

"You're William B. Travis?" he asked me.

He was a tall and soft-spoken fellow in his mid-fifties. He had grizzled gray hair and a chew of tobacco in his jaw. I liked him right off and thought I could possibly talk to him like a human being.

"Yes sir," I said.

"What one word did you hear tonight that shut you up like a clam?" he asked me. It was a funny question, but I liked it. I thought about it.

"'Nigger'," I said. "I was visiting a friend when this man and his son came knocking on the door with the butt of a forty-five. He was going to burn the house down around us if we didn't throw out a bag of gold."

"'Nigger'," he repeated. "'Bag of gold.' Be damned," he said.

"Truth, sir."

"I believe you. I don't think you boys had time to get any stories straight between you. Sandy bears all that out. So does his wife and kids and your lady friend. Even the neighbor saw you with the shotgun. Why'd you shoot him through the door?"

I looked into the man's eyes in the glaring bare porch light. He was waiting, weighing. I knew that I would have to make it real and good.

"I used to have a dog," I told him. "Good dog, gentle as he could be. But if I left the house and he somehow got out, he would terrorize the neighborhood and bite people."

"Yeah?"

"So the answer is, I don't know. I don't know why that good dog would do that. Maybe he was mad I was gone. Maybe not. The thing is, he would just do it. You asked me why I shot that man through the door. I won't say it was self-defense because that would be a lie. But what I will say is true to an extent, and that is: I don't know. I just don't know."

"All right, Mr. Travis. All right." He reached out and put his hand on my shoulder as if to comfort me. "One last question. What kind of shotgun do you have?"

"Winchester 12 gauge. Eight in the barrel, one in the chamber."

The Sheriff nodded. "You do know your gun. I have something to tell you, and I want you to listen to me, Mr. Travis."

"Bill," I said.

"Fine. Sometimes when a fellow kills another fellow, bad things begin to happen to him. I've seen it. I've seen it in the best and bravest of men. Their wits go south on them. They wind up tormenting themselves the way a bad tooth will torment a fellow if it isn't looked after until the fellow wishes he were dead just to relieve the pain. You seem like a nice fellow. What happened here was a terrible thing. Pretty terrible. And you got scared. You were protecting your friends and your lady friend. You shot through that door because of a miscommunication, you hear me? A man died because he was a plumb fool, you tracking with me? Yeah, you are. So when your conscience comes calling on you, remember to tell it those things. If you have any guns in your house, I'd get rid of them *before* it comes calling."

"Yes, sir," I said.

He stood back, looking at me, and I got the sense that he was slightly near-sighted.

"Seems like you want to ask me something," he said, his eyes probing even more deeply.

"I sure do," I said.

"Out with it."

"What was his name? The man I killed."

The Sheriff signed.

"Throckmorton," he said. "Terrance Throckmorton. A respected man around here. He ran the power plant."

"Oh," I said.

"I have something to tell you, Mr. Travis," the Sheriff said, and at that moment I realized I still didn't know his name.

"Yeah?"

"When my boys patted you down, they took everything you had out of your pockets, including your cell phone. About an hour ago it rang. Your wife. You're the proud father of a baby girl, seven pounds, three ounces."

And that's when I fainted.

CHAPTER SEVENTEEN

When I awoke on Sandy Jones' living room couch, the last person I expected to see was sitting in the easy chair next to me. I sat up. My head spun for a moment. Someone had told me something and then I remembered nothing after that.

"Oh," I said. "Hi, Mike."

"Hi yourself," he said.

"What's eating you?" I asked.

"I knew that if you got all mixed up in this, that people were going to die. My boss is dead."

"What does that make you?" I asked.

"I don't know. You mean in the company? We'll see."

Sandy Jones came into the living room and handed Mike Fields a cup of hot coffee.

"Thanks, Sandy," Mike said. "What are we going to do with Travis here?"

"What do you mean?" Sandy asked. "He's not under arrest."

"Tell me the truth, Sandy," Mike said. "Who really shot him? I buy that bullshit about coon hunting about as easy as I buy the conspiracy theory that the moon landing was faked."

"But it was," Sandy said.

"What?"

"Faked. The moon landing."

"Aw, shut up, Sandy," Mike said. He turned to me.

"I heard all about the bag of gold and the threat to burn the house down. I don't know what to believe. So maybe you'd better tell me everything, Bill."

I looked over at Sandy and he gave his head the very faintest of nods.

"All right," I said. "All I can tell you, Mike, is that this is about the hole, and what's not down there."

"What do you mean 'what's *not* down there?' The last time we talked about this it was about illegal dumping of nuclear waste."

"It's that, to be sure. And it's a whole lot more."

At that moment the screen door with its blast hole in the center banged open and the children rushed in, followed closely by Dotty Jones and Mary Jo.

"Daddy! Daddy!" The kids yelled.

"I'm all right, I'm fine. Hey!" His kids swarmed over him and he lifted the youngest into the air and she curled her fingers into his hair.

Dotty Jones came over to me, knelt down and kissed me hard on the cheek.

Mary Jo stood there, her hands on her hips. She wore a bright smile and a knowing smirk.

"What?" I asked her.

"You fooler," she said, and I felt warm inside. I was willing to bet it was the first time she had smiled since she'd gotten word of Brad's death.

I shrugged.

She came over to me and gave me a kiss on the other cheek.

"Congratulations," she whispered in my ear, and for a second my mind fogged up and I was in mystery as to what she was alluding to, then something from the back of my mind came to the front out of a veil of cobwebs. It was a face and a voice, speaking with the slightest East Texas drawl: *About an hour ago it rang. Your wife. You're the proud father of a baby girl, seven pounds, three ounces.*

"Oh," I said.

"You gonna pass out again, Bill?" Sandy asked.

"I'm fine," I said. "Got any more coffee?"

"I'll get it," Dotty said.

I noticed my wallet and cell phone sitting on the coffee table close by. I gathered them and flipped the phone open.

"Excuse me," I said. "I need to call my wife."

*****

The family retired to the kitchen and I was able to sit and talk with Julie in privacy for a few minutes.

She was doing fine. The baby was fine and perfect. She had a healthy set of lungs and there were no complications of any kind. Nat was there, but there was little reason for us to talk. He was doing his job with his niece, and my job as well. I'd have to personally thank him later.

The silences in our conversation said more about how Julie and I were than our words. They were intimate silences. Moments of sharing that would have to do in lieu of the fact that I wasn't actually there.

"You did good, Baby," I told her.

"*We* did good," she said.

"Yeah."

"Come home, Bill, as soon as you get things wrapped up there."

"I will."

"I heard there was a shooting," she said, finally. I'd known it was coming.

"Yeah."

"You okay?" she asked.

"I'm fine. I'm perfect, in fact."

"Yeah. I know. I can hear it in your voice. You sound like a happy father."

"I *am* a happy father."

"Okay. Good. I gotta go, Bill."

We said our goodbyes and hung up.

And it was then I realized I didn't even know my daughter's name.

*****

It had been bothering me since I'd first heard the name.

Throckmorton. Terry Throckmorton.

As I sat there alone on Sandy Jones' living room couch, a chatter of voices wafting through the house from the kitchen, I began to piece it all together.

I have often wondered about my mind, how it really works, or in many cases, doesn't. I observe everything, take it all in by osmosis, keep my eyes wide open when there is too little data, then shut them and pore over what has already come in when there is too much. It's only when I can separate it all out from my present environment that the pieces begin to fit themselves together to form some sort of coherent pattern. And when I do this, in those few instances when I have a quiet moment with which to examine, it usually comes together in a twinkling.

There had been an article in *CFO Magazine* about a lucky power plant manager that had a nose for finding gold mines. He had graduated from strip-mining to gold mining, and during his vacations had personally located three new gold mines in Central and South America, all within three months.

I don't have what is known as a photographic memory, but I believed the man's name was Throckmorton.

And there was something else besides, nagging at me, worrying me the way a bad itch will, until it's scratched. It was a feeling, and little more than that. Twice now I had heard the same line, something about being watched and about ghosts.

I shivered.

There it was. I looked around me at the Jones' living room, listened to the lyric voices from the kitchen and tried to place the feeling. It was a pit-of-the-stomach thing. Somewhere, somehow, I had turned the wrong corner. I had made the wrong decision. And someone else knew. And it wasn't Throckmorton, because he was dead.

I glanced at my watch. Straight up eleven o'clock p.m. Where had the time gone?

I got up and went into the kitchen. When there was a lull in the conversation, I interjected.

"Mary Jo. Time to get you home."

*****

I shook Sandy Jones' hand on the front porch, got a promise from him that he'd call me first thing in the morning before going to work and gave him my phone number.

Mike Fields followed me and Mary Jo out to my car.

"I can take her home, Bill," he said.

I glanced at Mary Jo, read her thoughts there on her face.

"No. That's okay, Mike. I brought her, so I'll take her back."

"Fine," he said. "I think you ought to head back to Austin now."

"I might just do that," I said, and as I said it, also knew there could be nothing further from the truth.

The traffic on Highway 30 had thinned down near non-existence and it was a long, quiet ride back to Mary Jo's, with little said between us.

CHAPTER EIGHTEEN

It was all wrong.

We both knew it the moment we rounded the curve and saw Mary Jo's place on the hill against the black trees in the brief wash of our headlights.

Freddie's pickup was there, but there wasn't a single light on in the place.

I stopped before her driveway on the edge of the bar ditch. Water stood there. There must have been one hell of a rain on this side of town.

"Sit tight, Darlin'," I told Mary Jo. "I'm going to make sure everything's all right up there."

"I want to go with you, Bill."

"No," I said. "If Brad were here, he wouldn't let you, and he'd be right about that. Lock your door."

She didn't bother replying to that. She knew I was right.

I stepped out, quickly closed the door behind me and started up the long, muddy driveway.

The darkness was very near complete.

*****

I moved slow, going from the mud and gravel of the drive into the wet grass where I could make less racket. I felt along the edge of Freddie's pickup, pausing to place a hand on the hood. Stone cold.

There is a feeling that creeps over one while trying to navigate in the dark. It's a distrust of anything and everything that may or may not be in the environment. It's an aloneness, and a cautiousness, as if at any moment and without warning, the dark will turn betrayer. And still there is another sense at work and at war with the first, and this is that the dark is also a protective barrier if there is the likelihood that another, unwelcome presence, is somewhere out there in the dark as well.

From memory I made the front steps. I counted in my head and felt for and found the three steps up, one after the other, then the less-solid and slight give of the front porch. I winced with each slow step to the front door, expecting a squeak that never came.

Behind the screen door the front door was wide open. I couldn't see this, but I could feel it and hear it. There was a quality of blackness about the doorway, a *yawningness* which had far more solidity about it than any cave a hundred feet underground, and also it seemed to absorb the sounds of the night: the slow, intermittent drip of water-soaked trees and brush, cars cutting through swaths of water along the highway in the distance, and seemingly my own breath and heartbeat.

I took my time opening the screen door, waiting for the beginning of a squeak or rattle that could give me away. Nothing.

I slipped through.

*****

I felt the presence the moment I stepped inside.

Someone was there inside the house, and they knew I was there as well. And it wasn't Freddie.

I moved a hand to the left wall slowly, touched it, then felt back behind the door, straining my arm to reach without moving the door, if it were at all possible.

My fingers groped until I found what I was searching for. Mary Jo's shotgun was there. Loaded? I had no way of knowing. Knowing her it was likely. Safety on? Maybe I could figure that one out by feel.

I tipped it toward me with one finger covering the hole of the barrel and it came away from the wall with only a faint whisper.

The other one hadn't heard. The other one, the knowing, waiting presence, was at least a room away and possibly further.

I hefted the shotgun in my hands, leveling it at the darkness and feeling for the safety. I found it, a small flat and round protrusion on the right side an inch behind and above the trigger guard, felt the circular groove in it. The safety was off. If I had to pull the trigger, I would hear a second gun blast that night — or nothing at all. It was the possibility of that 'nothing at all' that nearly unnerved me. I've never been any good with shooting dice, lottery tickets, slot machines, or other games of chance.

Holding the gun close to me so as not gouge anything with it and set up a racket, I took my first tentative steps into the room and very nearly blundered into the first trap that had been set for me.

My left wrist made contact with something and I flinched back, my breath caught in my throat.

I felt forward with my left hand and encountered the object. A chair — one of the kitchen chairs by the feel of it.

I stepped around it, slowly.

To my right should be a large sofa, an easy chair with an ottoman, a TV, but I no longer trusted the picture in my head of the inside of

Brad and Mary Jo's house. What's the old tasteless joke? If you want to drive a blind man crazy, re-arrange the furniture.

And that was it. I had hit on it.

This was a game, a very nasty game, and the opponent was nearby.

Five paces. Ten. I was in the hallway that led to the kitchen, my feelers out for the other presence.

The presence had moved, probably while I was messing around with the chair. It was to my left now, somewhere behind the wall that led from the kitchen and back bathroom through Mary Jo's bedroom.

We were circling each other.

A droplet of wetness struck my hand and I almost started. It was my own sweat. The room was cold and carried the strong odor of rain mingled with dusty window-screen, but I was sweating and my nerves were frayed to near the snapping point. My calf muscles were bunched and tightened, and if I didn't loosen up soon I would be seized by a bad leg cramp that might be my undoing.

The kitchen and another trap.

A lamp was there between the kitchen table and the stove. I bumped it and it fell forward, and in attempting to catch it, I pushed it forward even faster. It rattled, thumped and rolled and came to rest against the stove to my right. At the same time the house creaked and the faintest of footsteps moved quickly behind me from Mary Jo's room into the living room.

I quickly reached down and stood the lamp up where it had been and stepped toward the open back door and lodged myself behind the door.

The other was in the hallway.

He came on slowly, quietly.

My finger itched on the trigger. It jumped and moved, the tiniest of twitches. I realized I wasn't breathing and forced myself to exhale, slowly.

I paused before drawing a breath in, and heard the other's breath.

The presence stopped, a dozen feet away.

I opened my mouth all the way so as to breathe in silently and this worked.

He was there, just past the lamp.

My vision began playing tricks on me. My mind conjured a demonic smile there in the dark, the smile of a demented child perhaps, with an insect trapped in a jar upon which it planned to deal slow torture and study the effect.

There was a quiet noise from outside, not ten feet away.

"Bill?" Mary Jo's voice called out.

The other presence in the kitchen reacted instantly. It turned and ran down the hallway toward the living room.

"Mary Jo," I hissed, "stay right there. Don't move."

I didn't wait for a response, but ran across the room, knocked the lamp aside with yet another crash, and ran down the hallway toward the dimmest of lights from the front door. The screen door banged shut as I entered the living room.

I went out the front door at a dead run and could see nothing. I paused for a heartbeat, listening.

Distant wet smacking sounds, feet running over water-sogged ground to my right. There was a stand of trees there and the remains of a barbed-wire fence.

I ran in that direction and got a lance of pain in my right shoulder and nearly lost the shotgun. It spun me around and I nearly fell. It was a tree branch. If I had been a foot to the right it would have impaled my windpipe.

I stopped, took stock.

No sound. Nothing.

I waited two long minutes, then gave up and returned to Mary Jo.

*****

"Who was it?" Mary Jo asked.

"I dunno. He got away. Fast son of a bitch. Let's get the lights on and have a look inside."

"I'm scared, Bill," she said in the night.

"I've got your shotgun, Mary Jo."

"Bill?" she said.

"Yeah?"

"I'm sorry."

"About what?" I asked.

"I meant to load it," she said. "It's empty. The shells are in a box on the floor behind the front door."

So much for games of chance.

CHAPTER NINETEEN

The power had been turned off at the electrical box outside Mary Jo's bedroom window. Just a simple flip of a switch and the power was back on, but every indoor light had been turned off and every light-emitting device inside had been unplugged. Whoever had been there had wanted complete darkness.

Mud was tracked all through the house by a large pair of rubber-soled boots. He had come in the front door and had gone out the back and around again. The tracks led into the bedroom and bathroom and all over the small study area. Brad's papers were in disarray. No way to know what was missing.

Also, we found the worst when we came to Mary Jo's bedroom.

Freddie was dead.

His cold and naked form lay supine in the center of Mary Jo's bed. His eyes were still open, staring blankly at the ceiling. Also — and this was the worst part — there wasn't a single mark on his body.

*****

Mary Jo shed no tears. Neither did I.

Freddie was unlovable — had been as long as I'd known him. Possibly he had a friend — someone, somewhere who would shed a tear at the news of his death. But thus far I had not heard rumor of such a person.

A new set of county sheriff's officials and coroner's office officials were there and we began the rigamarole all over again.

I didn't mention anything about the shooting of Terry Throckmorton to the deputies. Mary Jo did her best to try to take as much heat off of me as she could, telling the first set of guys on the scene that she had been with me since we had left that afternoon to go see Brad's body at the hospital. The two deputies, a fellow named Jim Cook and one named Lawson Cooper, were no more than reserve deputies — guys who wore a badge and a gun but who were deputy sheriffs for their own jollies, drawing down no pay. I'd done a stint of that myself once, before I figured out that I didn't care much for busting people.

"Look, Mr. Travis," Deputy Cook said as Deputy Cooper dropped a sheet over Freddie's cold body in the next room. The door was still open. "Doesn't it strike you as a little odd that we got two dead brothers here in two days?"

"I'd say more like two and a half days," I said. "And be respectful of the missus here, please." I gestured toward Mary Jo.

"Sorry, ma'am," Cook said. "But still. You'd better tell me what's going on."

"If I knew, I'd tell you," I said, and no sooner than the words were out of my mouth that I remembered the journal under the front seat of my car. Were some of the answers there? That was a long shot. I itched to have a look at it.

"Oh boy," Lawson said, "here comes the cavalry."

Out the front window there were several sets of headlights and red and blue flashers coming up the driveway.

*****

We stood outside on Mary Jo's front porch. Mary Jo was inside, sitting down. She wouldn't talk to anybody. I was hoping to get a chance to talk to her soon. She'd been through enough shocks, and I didn't want anyone needling her. At the very least I'd coached her to sit and stay quiet and just watch.

The sheriff was there, a slim woman with the unlikely name of Larrabeth Williams, the first black female sheriff in one of the most conservative counties in the state. Her rise to local power had made national headlines when the incumbent sheriff had dropped dead of a massive heart attack two weeks after the primaries. No other conservative had run against him in the primaries, and Ms. Williams was the Democratic candidate. The Republicans had sued to have the election overturned and the Democrats had counter-sued. One minute she was a shoo-in, the next minute she was out, and a senior deputy was running for the sheriff's spot with the weight of most of the local establishment behind him. Then, three days before the election the issue had made it all the way to the Supreme Court where it took all of fifteen minutes to reverse everything.

Larrabeth Williams was the only name on the ticket other than the Independent, and she won ninety-five percent of the votes in one of the lowest voter-turnout elections in the county's history. The *Texas Monthly* had done a full article on her, complete with posed photos of Ms. Williams jogging and wearing American flag running shorts. Julie loved the picture and had put it in her scrap book.

"Do I know you?" she asked me.

A moth flittered around the porch light above us.

"No ma'am," I said. "But I know you."

"Oh. *Texas Monthly?"* she asked.

"Yes ma'am."

"Shoot. I never jogged a day in my life, and I didn't even jog that day. It was all put-up."

"Yes, ma'am," I said.

"Why is there a dead man in there?"

"Somebody killed him," I said.

She looked at me with disbelieving eyes, then rolled them.

"Good Lord. I know *that.* What I want to know is why and who."

"I know you do," I said.

"I got a call on the way over here. Somebody recognized your name over the police radio."

"Oh," I said.

"You shot a man just a few hours ago."

"Seems like last week," I said.

"Tell me what happened."

I explained it, or did my best without overtly lying to her. I let her believe what she wanted to believe. Then she surprised the hell out of me when I was done.

"You may fool other people, Mr. Travis, but you aren't fooling this girl. Sandy Jones shot and killed Throckmorton. And you were there and decided to protect him. He's not supposed to have a gun, so you made it your gun and got your stories all straight so that Sandy wouldn't go back to prison because he's got more children than God. How am I doing so far?"

"Well... I — ."

"That's just what I thought. You listen to me, William B. Travis. This is my county. I didn't think I'd win and I didn't want to. It was sort of like Nichelle Nichols landing that role on *Star Trek*. It was the last thing I wanted, but now I've got to do it. So you and your lady friend are going to take a little ride with me and we're going to sort all this out. You're going to tell me everything, and I mean everything."

I studied her face. She was all of thirty years old and she wore a thick Kevlar vest underneath her brown uniform, likely to protect her from everybody, not just criminals. Her face was a creamy chocolate color and her eyes seemed to be a pupil-less black. She was stern and hard on the exterior, but I had the notion that kittens, small babies, old people and invalids could make her melt. And I found myself admiring the hell out of her.

"How'd you know so quick about Sandy Jones?"

"He's my cousin," she said.

I laughed.

"Fine," I said. "Let's go."

*****

I retrieved the journal from under my front seat, locked my car and went in and spoke briefly with Mary Jo. I explained to her that the sheriff was waiting and that I trusted her. She gave me a smile and took my hand.

CHAPTER TWENTY

We were in the Sheriff's cruiser parked off the shoulder of the highway a mile from Mary Jo's house.

She turned her engine off and rolled her window down. Her police radio continued to squawk away. I waited, listening to the night. Larrabeth reached over and turned off her radio.

"Well?" she said.

"You have to know how a company is put together," I began, and over the next hour told her everything I knew.

*****

"This is written in French, Bill," Larrabeth said. "Nobody writes like this anymore. Not even in France."

"You can read French?" I asked.

"Yes. I took it high school, then two semesters of it in college before switching my major to social work."

"Where'd you go to school?" Mary Jo asked her from the rear seat.

"Prairie View A&M. I'm a black female. Where else would I go to college in this state? I didn't have the grades for Ivy League, and Prairie View is sixty miles from here."

"Oh," Mary Jo said.

Larrabeth flipped through the journal with care. The pages were brittle, ancient.

"Is there a date?" I asked.

"Yep."

"Please give it a try."

"Oh, I don't have to try. I can read this stuff."

I sat back in the shotgun seat of the Sheriff's cruiser and waited. A glance at my watch revealed the hour: 2:40 a.m. Somewhere in a hospital room, my wife was holding my new born baby girl.

"'From the journal of Louis du Orly, Master, *Le Royale.*' This entry says 'July 16, 1673'."

I whistled.

"'Today *Le Royale* was driven upon the shoals of the Brazos de Dios by the Devil Wind, and here we removed the contents of the hold. She is being stripped naked of anything we may need in the coming weeks and months, perhaps years ahead.' What's this about, Bill? This thing is nearly four-hundred years old."

"I know," I said. "I saw a cave painting of the ship with these two eyes, down near where they keep the spent nuclear core rods."

"Remind me to get someone to check you out with a Geiger-counter," she said.

"Please," I said. "Keep reading."

"'A party of savages has been watching us from the far shore. They are almost...' what's this word... I think — "phantoms, but I sense their eyes, watching our every movement. Perhaps we merely puzzle them. It is to be hoped they are not cannibals, as those of the coast of Corpus Christi.'"

"He's referring to Karankawa Indians," Mary Jo said. "Texas' coastal cannibals. They were some of the first encountered."

"Shit," Larrabeth said.

"Keep reading," Mary Jo said.

"'"Three of the men have died with the falling sickness. They were hardy veterans of our campaigns against the Spaniards, and were buried in shallow mud graves which we have covered with stones to keep the wild animals from defiling them. There are shrieks in the night the like of which I have never heard. It chills the blood. The Devil Storm has passed away to the north of us, and now the wind which was once behind us blows in our faces and the rains will not stop.'

"That's all for that date."

"Please," I said, "don't stop now."

"Next entry, 'July 20, 1673. The way home is barred. There is a huge wall of mud between us and the sea. I have burned the ship to the water line. There is no going home. There is only this place and the wild lands ahead.'"

"Okay," I said. "More?"

"Yeah. A lot more. 'August 1, 1673. I believe today is the first of August. Somewhere I have lost a day, perhaps two. The ship is gone, and I cannot bear the sight of her ribs sticking up from the mud. We have moved our encampment into the forest along the bank and have set up lean-tos. The mosquitoes are fierce. The savages have approached us, bringing food. They wish peace, and peace I will give them. I will attempt to learn the language of this strange people. They tap their chests and say "Noffa-sot". It may mean "man", or "leader", or the name of their clan. I have gestured towards them and said "Nava-sotta" and "friend", and thump my heart, to which they reply "tay-has", and smile. We are saved.'"

"They found the Navasota Indians. That was luck," I said.

"Yeah," Larrabeth said and flipped another page. "There's more here. And this next entry looks like a doozy."

CHAPTER TWENTY-ONE

During the two months following the storm that stranded them, Louis du Orly, the survivors of his crew and half a dozen imprisoned Spanish trekked deep into the heart of an East Texas forest of unimaginable extent, and there at the center of a great encampment of natives, homes were constructed for them and they settled down to live out their lives.

Louis took a Navasota squaw as his wife and lived there for another ten years.

In 1681, the journal was penned in a different hand, that of Le Fitte. The captain had begun to go mad. He babbled and raved about impending invasions from the Aztecs and from the Spaniards, about gold and jewels and the hunt to find him, and about a "blue bone".

Le Fitte's scant and cryptic hand detailed his Captain's last days, filled with madness and severe fevers, from which he would never recover.

The final entry stated simply "Summer 1683", and preserved du Orly's final words: "The blue bone is possessed by the spirits of all who touch it. It feeds on their desires, their greed, and therefore must be buried deep in the earth. This is my last command to you, noble son. Bury it. Bury it deeply."

Le Fitte carried out his master's command in that final entry, consigning the blue bone, the body of the Captain, and his immense yet worthless treasure "in the grotto of the gods beneath the land," where it would never be seen again by mortal eyes.

"They sealed the hole," I said.

"Yes," Larrabeth replied.

"But CTL&P found it," Mary Jo said.

"Sandy Jones found it," I said.

There followed a silence that lasted whole minutes.

"Bill," Larrabeth said finally, handing me the journal, "this should be in a museum. It's worth quite a bit."

"I know," I said. "I'll make sure it finds its way to safe-keeping. But only after the cleanup."

"Right," she said. "We've got to get those damned core rods disposed of. That son of a bitch Throckmorton. I don't hate people too easily, but I'll tell you, if anybody deserved killing, it was him."

I could have easily commented, but I kept my mouth shut. It's too easy to speak ill of someone after they're dead and gone, especially if you didn't know them personally. I was at least happy about the fact that I'd never gotten to know Terry Throckmorton. Larrabeth's tone was all I needed to hear to convince me that had I known him, I would likely have echoed her comments.

"Brad knew," Mary Jo said. "It was what he couldn't tell me."

"Yes," I said. "I think he did. And Sandy knew as well. And someone else, other than Terry Throckmorton and the drivers that brought those core rods in."

"Who?" Mary Jo asked.

I allowed the question to hang there in the air for a moment. I turned to face Larrabeth Williams.

"Ma'am," I said.

"Yeah?" Larrabeth said.

"When Mary Jo called me to tell me about Brad's death, she said he was murdered."

"That's right," Mary Jo said from the rear seat. "I knew it then and I know it even more now."

"And with his brother, Freddie dead now, and not a mark on him, just like Brad..."

Larrabeth sighed. She looked straight ahead, out into the night. Or perhaps she was looking inward, examining herself.

"This," she began, "is a double-murder investigation."

Larrabeth turned in her seat to face Mary Jo.

"Ma'am," she said. "I'm going to find the man who killed your husband and your brother-in-law, I promise you. And when I do, I'm going to make sure he wishes he was never born."

CHAPTER TWENTY-TWO

It was 6:00 a.m. and the sun was threatening to rise through a scudding of low clouds to the east.

I took Mary Jo back into town with me and ensconced her in the hotel where I'd stayed in the night before. My room was next door to hers, just a rap on the wall away if I were needed.

I slept fitfully, until I got a knock on my door at a quarter till noon. I was sure it was Mary Jo.

"Heidi!"

"Hi, Bill," she said, holding a small clutch purse primly in front of her. She wore a light-yellow sun dress and her hair was gussied up. I rubbed sleep out of my eyes.

"Can I come in?" she asked.

"Sure," I said, and held the door open for her. "There's a chair. I'll sit on the bed."

"You haven't changed clothes," she said.

"Too tired."

"Busy night?"

"You could say that," I said. "What's up?"

"It's Mike. He's got funny ideas in his head. He's says you might be a loose cannon. That you're running around either getting people killed or killing them yourself. What's going on?"

"Heidi," I began, then didn't know how to continue. I wanted to tell her that she was out of her depth, that she was better off not knowing things. Really, I wanted her to leave so I could crash for another eight hours.

"Bill," she said. "My husband is going... I feel like he's losing his mind. His best friend is dead, and now his best friend's brother is dead, his boss is dead, and I want to know what the hell is going on." She said all of it quietly, as if she knew a raised voice might bring unwanted attention.

"Mary Jo's next door," I said. "Thank you for not shouting."

"I couldn't shout at you, Bill. I... I like you."

What else was there to say? "I like you too, Heidi."

"At one time you said it differently. The word wasn't 'like.'"

"I know," I said. "I know. It was a long time ago. A lifetime."

"Maybe. Not so long for me, though. I don't have many friends, Bill. Mike doesn't like for me to have friends."

"I'm sorry for you, Heidi," I said. I began itching for a way to get her to leave.

"Don't say that," she said.

I faced her. "Heidi," I said. "You live in another world. A bubble world. You always have. Everything you've ever needed was given to you on a silver platter. When I knocked on your door once back in high school, do you know who answered? Your maid. Do you know who she was? She was my seventh grade history teacher. She left education, a thing she loved more than anything, because she could make more money working for your parents."

"Don't be mean, Bill," she said, quietly.

"I'm not being mean, I'm being real. You're a fine woman. You've got a good husband, who also makes good money. You've got a big house with a sculptured lawn and a Japanese tea garden I wouldn't mind having. No, I'm not actually jealous, it's just that I'm exhausted and I don't have time for this. Tell Mike to chill. I've got everything under wraps. I'm closing in on Brad's killer."

"But you still need friends," she said.

"I've got friends. Friends in places you've never dreamed of, both high and low."

"I'm leaving." She stood, stared down at me for a moment, her teeth biting her lower lip. For a moment I thought she was going to slap me.

She turned toward the door.

"Go home, Heidi," I said.

She walked out the door without a word and slammed it behind her.

*****

I couldn't get back to sleep.

I went down to my car, fished around in my trunk until I came up with the suit bag I was hoping was still there. I hadn't seen it since I'd brought the car back from West Texas and a visit to a Texas Ranger friend the previous spring.

I was in luck. Inside there was a set of clothes, including a pink shirt purchased for me by Julie that I swore I'd never wear. But what the hell? Only real men can wear pink and get away with it.

Back upstairs and into the shower I let the water scald and sting me until I began to come back to life.

I dressed and tapped lightly on Mary Jo's door. She answered, looking refreshed.

"Take me home, Bill. I've got to get my car. There's a memorial service for Brad today at three."

"Sure."

*****

It bothered me, prodded at me until the moment Mary Jo asked me to stand up and say a few words about Brad. There, two rows behind Mary Jo were Mike and Heidi. What I was thinking of that whole time was: "What in the hell is a blue bone?"

We were under a small pavilion in Astin Park, a stone's throw from Lake Bryan, the same lake I'd once fallen into as a child during a school picnic. Brad had been there, laughing his ass off at me before helping to pull me out. The pavilion hadn't existed then. I looked down at Mary Jo, then at Mike and Heidi, then across the many waiting faces until I picked out Larrabeth Williams and a deputy seated in the back row.

I gave them all a smile and began. I told them stories of Brad and me — some of the off-the-wall stunts he'd pulled during the many years I'd known him. I had them alternately laughing and tearing-up, as I went from a very Brad-like antic to something he'd once told me during one of his more poignant moments. I let the weight of the words carry out over the audience, and a silence flowed back to me.

And then I felt it.

A chill went through me.

He was there, the presence from the dark house.

Among the thirty or so of us, he was sitting there, his eyes boring into me as they had tried to do through the inky blackness of Mary Jo's kitchen.

I scanned the faces, trying to be natural and yet deliberate, but my search turned up nothing.

I decided to leave off with a few words of comfort for Mary Jo, telling her that I knew Brad had loved her more than anyone or anything, but then it came to me. There was an opportunity here.

"Mary Jo," I said, turning to her. "We will find him... the person that did this to Brad, and to Freddie. We *will* get him. I promise you."

I had the complete attention of every person there. The attention was palpable, solid.

Mary Jo nodded at me, mouthed a heart-felt "thank you" to me, and then wiped the tears from her eyes with a wadding of Kleenex.

"Brad," I said, looking slightly up and past the crowd, "I'm sorry. I'm sorry I wasn't here for you when you needed me most. You were my oldest friend, and I will miss you. I'll get him, Brad." I dropped my gaze level again and looked, waiting for a sign of any kind. A look, a shudder, a flinch. Anything.

One last look, meeting steady gazes.

"I'll get him," I said softly, and knew that every person there heard me perfectly, including *him.*

The cool breeze had died completely. Stillness. Not a sound, not a movement.

I was done. I stepped away from the small lectern and sat down beside Mary Jo.

She squeezed my hand and then stood, turning to take in the crowd.

"Thank you Bill, for those kind words," she said. "And thank you all for coming. I feel like Brad is here, watching us, and that he is pleased with your attendance here. Please join with us in singing Amazing Grace."

We all stood and Mary Jo led us in a strong and clear voice.

And I wept hot, fierce tears, for all the good it did me to resist.

CHAPTER TWENTY-THREE

Mike and Heidi came up to me after the ceremony as the crowd dispersed. Heidi chatted with Mary Jo and Mike pulled me aside.

"That was either very smart or very stupid," he said, but he was smiling. "You've put the fear of God in somebody, hopefully."

"Thanks," I said. I noticed Sheriff Williams standing in the sunlight at the edge of the pavilion, watching people file back to their cars. She looked my way and dropped me a wink and shook her head in the negative. No likely suspects, that meant.

"You and Mary Jo are welcome to join us for dinner," Mike said.

Mary Jo must have overheard. She came over with Heidi in tow and said: "I can't accept." She turned to me. "I'm leaving, Bill. I'm leaving town, right this minute. I won't be back."

"Mary Jo," I began, but she cut me off with a nod of her head.

She threw her arms around me and hugged me tightly and whispered in my ear.

"See that they bury Brad's body properly. Then go back to your family. Your wife needs you right now."

"I've got to —"

"I know. You made a promise and I know you'll keep it. But for now, do what's right for you. You've done all you can for me and for Brad, except to see he's buried. I can't do that, myself. I have to go. I won't be calling you, Bill. Don't call me. I have to start life over again. Please understand. I promised Brad I'd go, remember?"

She regarded me close-up, her eyes probing mine. They were clear and bright and full of life. Brad was gone from her, now. A great weight had been lifted.

I nodded to her, understanding her fully.

"Go, Mary Jo. Live life."

"Take care of yourself, Bill Travis," she said. "I love you."

She kissed me tenderly on the cheek, then she was away and walking toward her car. I stood there and watched her go. She never looked back.

"Well," Heidi said, and left it at that.

*****

I had an uncomfortable lunch with Mike and Heidi. I had other fish to fry at the moment, but it was something I couldn't get out of unless I wanted to turn the couple into complete enemies.

We dined at a posh restaurant, a private club on the top floor of a bank building, blocks from my old high school.

"Bill," Mike said. "I'll make sure they bury Brad with some respect. I feel responsible for him. I tried to warn him to leave well enough alone. You go back to Austin."

I thought about it. Julie and our baby were waiting for me.

"Thanks, Mike," I said. "I'll consider it."

"Bill," Heidi began, but Mike looked hard at her. "Nothing."

"I have a feeling," Mike said, "if you don't go, then you might be sorry."

"Are you threatening me?" I asked him. "That won't work."

"I'm not threatening you, you prick. I'm advising you. I don't want to read about you in the papers, that's all."

"I feel like you know something and you're not telling me."

He began cutting his *filet mignon*. Heidi took a sip of wine and tried to appear as though she were looking at something outside the window. The only thing out there was city skyline.

"Look," I said. "Brad's dead. So is Freddie. Terry Throckmorton's dead. Mary Jo's gone from town. That narrows down the playing field a whole lot."

"Why did you bring the Sheriff in on this, then, if it's so simple?" Mike asked.

"She brought herself in. This is a double-murder." I'd had enough. "Look. I've got to go. I'll let you do something good. You've got the pull and you've got the money. Bury Brad when they release his body. I'm leaving for Austin."

"When?" Heidi asked.

"Right now."

I got up, opened my wallet, fished out a hundred dollar bill and laid it on the table.

"I hope that covers lunch," I said, then turned and stalked out.

CHAPTER TWENTY-FOUR

He was waiting for me at the same intersection as before.

Red and blue lights flashed at me in my rearview mirror.

"Aw hell," I said.

I pulled over and stopped, rolled my window down. It was hot out, a traditional Texas summer outdoor oven, the temperature set on 'Broil'.

I stayed put and waited. After a minute a familiar face grinned down at me.

"Hello, William."

"Hello, Officer Leonard."

"I thought you weren't supposed to be here."

"I'm not. Just leaving."

"Good. I'll escort you."

"That's not necessary," I said.

"I'll just do you this one last favor," he said.

"Thanks a million."

CHAPTER TWENTY-FIVE

I was home with Julie, our new daughter, Jennifer, and our adopted daughter, Jessica.

Jessica surprised us both by taking time out of her social schedule — which, for a thirteen year-old seemed of late to be busier than some child movie stars — to help with the baby. To hear Jessica put it, she could have used a handful of booking agents and still not gotten everything done. But to see her hold the baby and dance around our bedroom, smiling down at little Jenny and kissing her little forehead for the five-hundredth time, well, let me tell you, this father felt no small measure of pride.

Julie seemed to be pleased with me as well. Possibly it had something to do with my coming home so soon. She didn't ask me any questions about Brad or Mary Jo, didn't comment when she knew I was still trying to sort it all out, and didn't trade verbal jabs with me the way we usually did. I would have to say she was pleased with herself. And she should have been. Jennifer was beautiful.

I got the call on a Saturday afternoon while Julie and I watched a rare movie together and Jessica was changing the baby.

"Hello?"

"Bill Travis?" I recognized the voice. Husky, female. A certain East Texas Sheriff.

"Yes, Sheriff."

"You must have caller-ID," she said.

"Or I must recognize your voice."

"All right. I'm calling about Sandy Jones."

"Your cousin," I said.

"Yeah. Him. He's gone crazy, Bill. I need your help."

*****

Another long highway trip and therefore another chance to go over everything that had happened, uninterrupted.

I remembered Mary Jo kissing me on the cheek and turning away, leaving for good. A presence in the pitch blackness, probing for me. Flashlights roving over ancient cavern wall etchings. An empty grotto. A promise to Mary Jo and to Brad and the assembled mourners. The knowledge that the killer was right there, looking directly at me.

I ate up hot summer miles like so much sticky taffy.

I skirted Bryan this time. There were going to be no run-ins with Officer H. Leonard if I had anything to say about it.

A late evening sun found me parked in Mary Jo's driveway.

The house had that empty look about it. It is amazing to me how quickly a place goes south when there is no one around to imbue it with life. It looked lonely. Desolate and cast-off.

Possibly I'd find Brad's ghost in there and maybe we'd finally get a chance to talk.

I sat for fifteen minutes, just looking at the place. Then, with an empty feeling in the pit of my stomach, got out of my car and walked up.

*****

The front and back doors were locked. The windows were either locked tight or painted shut. I scanned the horizon, noting an absence of traffic along the highway. I went around back, found a good-sized stone in the weeds and stove in the lowest window.

Standing on top of one of the picnic table benches, I cleared away as much glass as possible and managed to get the window frame raised.

I went inside.

The electricity was off and the interior was gloomy. I moved from the kitchen down the long hallway to the living room and stopped in front of Brad's desk.

There were stacks of papers, neatly arranged, books on electromagnetic field theory. Leafing through these I noted complex mathematical equations and chicken-scratches in Brad's own hand in the margins. Comments like: "not true!" and "so it is thought." I dropped the book on the floor beside the desk and the echo throughout the house gave me a brief case of the chills.

The next book down was an exhaustive treatise on the high-frequency patents of Nicola Tesla. Many of the pages were dog-eared and there were even more hand-written notations in Brad's hand. I couldn't make heads or tails of any of it. I dropped the book with the other on the floor.

I sat in Brad's chair and began going through his desk.

*****

I knew who the killer was.

It had come over me while on my way back to Austin two weeks previously, what seemed like a lifetime ago. It had shaken me so badly that I had to stop the car at a roadside park and listen to the moan of the cicadas and crickets and the drone of the passing cars and trucks.

What I didn't know was how. And why.

And I was determined to answer those two questions before I made my move.

*****

In the left-hand bottom drawer of Brad's desk, behind a stack of books that had to be removed one by one, I found it.

A tape recorder wrapped in a set of blueprints and held together with a large rubber band.

There was a tape inside, cued up, ready to go. The batteries were still fresh.

Sitting there in Brad's chair in his empty house, in his lost world, I listened. And the longer I listened, the madder I got.

CHAPTER TWENTY-SIX

I left in the near darkness, locking the front door behind me. I'd have to come back in the near future and do something about the kitchen window. For the time-being, I had fish to fry.

*****

The Brazos County Sheriff's Department is on the ground floor of the six-story Court House building, which houses most of the county departmental head offices, including the County and District Courts. The upper three floors of the building are all jail.

I was buzzed through an inner door by a uniformed girl sitting behind a bullet-proof enclosure who looked like she should still be in high school. She looked bored beyond all patience, but when I smiled, she smiled back.

Larrabeth Williams greeted me and I followed her back to her office.

"Let me get a few things, Bill, then we can go. You're riding with me."

"Fine," I said.

I watched and waited as Larrabeth gathered up a closed file box and a box of zip-lock bags, the kind used for evidence. I wondered.

I offered to carry the box and she let me. There was no adornment to the box, no tell-tale scribbles on it to give me a clue what was inside.

It was heavy, though, and felt like papers — about seven or eight reams worth.

"What's this?" I asked, as we walked out the back door of the Sheriff's Office and into her private garage.

"Business records," she said. "Had hell getting them. It took a court order."

"The power company?" I asked.

She smiled at me and opened the trunk. I deposited the box and wiped the sweat from my brow.

We climbed inside and she started up the engine, switched on the police radio and reported to dispatch she was leaving. I recognized the code: "Out of Service."

"You're one smart white boy," she said. "Damn right it's power company records."

"Who are we going after?" I asked.

She backed out of the garage and into the street. Larrabeth cranked up the air conditioning.

"First, we're going to see Sandy."

"And then?" I asked.

"That's up to you," she said.

*****

I knew from the direction of our travel that we weren't heading to Sandy and Dorothy Jones' home.

"What gives?" I asked her.

She turned to me.

"You give," she said. "Starting now. Two weeks ago when you left town without telling me, there were a few things we didn't cover. We talked about core rods and everything in the du Orly journal — which we both agree needs to be in a museum somewhere — and about your little trip down there with Sandy and that he took a bag of gold but everything else, including the skeletons, are missing. But a whole lot we didn't cover. You held out on me."

"What do you want to know?" I asked her.

"Who killed Brad Fisher and why and how? Who killed his brother and why and the same how? You see, the why is not the same why in those two cases."

I sighed.

"Talk," she said.

"It's all on a tape."

"What tape?"

"Brad's tape. It was on a tape recorder in the bottom desk drawer of his desk. His confession to me or to whoever else found the tape. It's in my car, along with the journal and Brad's mechanical drawings of how to re-create the blue bone. What it does and how it does it."

"Anything else there?" she asked me.

"I said it was a confession. It's an admission of something I already knew."

"Like what?"

"Like who killed him. And why."

"Shit," she said.

"Exactly."

"I want to hear that tape. We have to make copies. It's evidence."

"It's not exactly a dying declaration, but..."

"It's close enough," she said. "Anything else?"

"One thing," I said. "The Chief of Police is Mike Fields' father. You know him?"

"Sure I do," she said, and raised an eyebrow.

"I'll bet Mike's name is all over those CTL&P records."

"It is."

"And his father?"

"You know a lot for a skinny white man," she said.

"I thought so. Do you know an Officer H. Leonard of the Bryan Police Department?"

She whistled.

"Thought so again," I said.

"Mike killed Brad Fisher?"

"No," I said.

"He had Harvey Leonard do it?"

"No."

"I want to hear that tape," she said. "Anything else you want to tell me right now?"

"Not at the moment."

"Fine," Larrabeth said. "But you'll have to spill the rest of it soon. We're here."

*****

To take a line from Alcoholics Anonymous, the Brazos County Mental Health and Mental Retardation is its own higher power. It runs what is known as "residential treatment centers" throughout the twin cities. The Residential Treatment Center to which Sandy Jones had been taken was a two-story orange-brick house on the west side of Bryan. The first floor windows had black wrought iron bars on them, not so well-hidden by overgrown ficus and oleander. The second floor windows were likely nailed shut. Once inside, there was no way out except the front or back door.

We pulled up in front and walked across a yard that was weeks overdue for mowing.

The front door was locked. Larrabeth rang the doorbell.

A pair of eyes and arched eyebrows appeared in one of three high and narrow front door window panes.

"Open up," Larrabeth said.

A key rattled in the front door. It opened.

"Yes?" the male attendant in blue nursing scrubs asked.

"Sandy Jones," she said. "I want to see him. Right now."

"Uh. Um." The attendant stood there, his eyes shifting around.

"Better get a move on," I said. "The last person that said 'Uh' and 'Um' to her winded up in a holding cell with fifty gang rapists."

"Uh. Um. This... this way."

He closed the door behind us, turned the key in the lock, then dropped the grungy elastic necklace holding it back around his neck.

We followed him up a flight of stairs and to the second floor. A strange, heavy-set woman in her early fifties walked toward us, then past. She held curled hands out before her and shook as though she had an ague. Her expression was mindless.

"You're looking at their product here," I whispered to Larrabeth as she turned to watch the woman pass.

"Shit," she said.

The orderly stopped before an open door, pointed limply inside.

Larrabeth glanced in the room and at the strait-jacketed form on the bed, then told the orderly: "Scat."

The fellow scatted.

Sandy Jones had seen better days. I was amazed at the difference two weeks could make in a person.

He lay there, staring up at the ceiling with blinkless eyes. He mumbled something, the same thing, over and over.

"Jesus," Larrabeth said.

I knelt down beside him and whispered in his ear.

"Sandy," I said. "Wherever you are, I need your help."

He blinked, once. The soundless words failed on his lips. His body relaxed. I wondered how long he had been tense.

I waited. A minute passed. Two.

I looked at Larrabeth.

"Ma'am," I said. "I'm going to have to say something not very nice to him. I'm apologizing in advance."

"Go ahead and do it," she said.

The house was still and quiet but for a distant repeated dull thump on a wall somewhere.

"Sandy? What do you say when they come knocking on your door and threaten to burn the niggers out?"

He blinked, a thrum of eye bats faster than a person could count. Then he turned slowly toward me.

"Don't... threaten... my *FAMILY!*"

"Right," I said. "Sandy. I'm going to count from five to one and snap my fingers. When I do you will be fully awake and aware. Five. Four. Three. Two. One."

I snapped my fingers in front of his face.

His body jerked. He sat up, fast.

"What the shit?" he said.

"Sweet Jesus," Larrabeth breathed.

"Bill?" he asked, his face forming the saddest frown I believe I have ever seen.

"It's me," I said. "You're in a psych ward. We're getting you out of here."

"My God," Sandy said. "It was terrible. Oh my Lord." His eyes probed mine, begging for understanding.

"They've got it," he said quietly.

"Got what?" Larrabeth asked.

"The blue bone."

CHAPTER TWENTY-SEVEN

We made quick work of the strait jacket.

Sandy walked between us. We went down the long hall and the stairs. The orderly was waiting in the foyer by the front door.

"Uh. You... He can't —"

"Unlock that door," Larrabeth said.

"Uh. Can't... uh, do that."

"Fine," she said.

I knew what was coming long before she went through the motions.

Sheriff Larrabeth Williams pulled out her Smith & Wesson service revolver, aimed it at the front door lock and fired. The door knob and the lock mechanism blew outward into the night with a crash. The door drifted back on its hinges, as if welcoming us to leave. A curl of blue smoke hung in the air. The house had gone completely quiet. My ears rang.

"Thank you," she told the orderly, who was flat against the wall and as white as a ghost. "I've been wanting to fire this thing ever since they gave me this damned badge."

She turned to Sandy and me and smiled.

"Come on," she said.

*****

You have to know how a company is put together...

Mike Fields had said that.

Who better to run everything than the man that knows everything?

"Tell me where we're going, Bill?" Larrabeth said.

"The hole," Sandy said from the rear seat.

Larrabeth turned and looked at him. They exchanged some kind of silent communication.

"Who among your deputies do you trust the most?" I asked the Sheriff.

"There's only two of them. You've met them. Jim Cook and Lawson Cooper."

"The reserve deputies that were the first to Mary Jo's?" I said.

Larrabeth nodded.

"Get one or both of them on your cell phone. No police radio for this one."

"We'll need Hot Papa suits," Sandy said.

"What?" Larrabeth said.

"Anti-radiation suits," I said. "Lead-lined with leaded glass."

"We've got some of those in the fallout shelter below the court house. They're pretty old."

"They'll have to do," I said. "Can Cook or Cooper get them?"

"I think so. Let me make the call."

We wended our way through night traffic and out towards the edge of town as the Sheriff made her calls.

"They'll meet us there," she said finally.

"I don't have my key anymore," Sandy said.

Larrabeth and I exchanged knowing glances.

"That's all right," I said. "Larrabeth's got one."

We waited at the gate for an hour before the county cruiser pulled off the road. During that time I had my chance to get a few things out in the open between me and Sandy Jones. Larrabeth stood there between us, as if listening to the night. To her credit she never said a word.

"Why did you do it, Sandy?" I asked him.

"How much to you know?"

"Everything," I said.

He sighed, then began.

"We thought you would be happy with just the journal," he said. "Then, when Throckmorton came and... I shot him through the door, I was really protecting my family."

"In more ways than one," I said. "You were protecting them also from your lie."

"I had to," he said.

"What are you going to tell Dotty?" I asked him.

"If I tell her... she'll divorce me. We won't..." Sandy choked and broke down into a brief fit of tears. "We won't be a family anymore. Not without Dotty. I'll be back in prison inside of six months. If I go back there, I'll kill myself. I'll do it."

"You're not going back to prison," I told him. "You didn't kill Brad. You didn't kill his brother. You didn't even know who did it."

I allowed him to get the hard, festering lump that he had been holding onto out where he could look at it. The truth, though painful, I've found, is always best.

"I have to tell her?" he asked.

"You have to, Sandy," I said.

"It'll never be the same between us."

"No. But in many ways it will be better. At least there won't be a lie between the two of you and between you and your own children. Brad had the same lie going. He couldn't face it. And now he's dead and gone."

"I'll try," he croaked. "God help me, I'll try."

"I'll help you," I said. "I know the duress you've been under. She'll understand."

"You don't know my woman, Bill," he said, his tears beginning to dry. He was beginning to accept it: To step to the right side of the curtain he had drawn between himself and his own world.

"Maybe I don't," I said. "But I know people. They're good. Almost all of them are basically good."

"Yeah," he said, and wiped his eyes with his sleeve. "Almost all."

Almost, I thought. I wished it could be different from that, not for the first or the last time.

*****

Deputies Cook and Cooper climbed out of their cruiser and joined us.

"We need a warrant to go in there," Lawson Cooper said.

"Got it, right here," Larrabeth said, and hefted her pistol.

I turned to Cook and Cooper. "I have reason to believe," I began, "that if we don't move now, then the evidence we're looking for will be long gone by the time we get back. There's no time for a warrant."

"Oh," Cook said. "Then what are we waiting for?"

Flame coughed from a gun in the night. The gate lock was massive and tough. It took three shots from Larrabeth's revolver before the lock flew away into the high weeds.

We followed the narrow roadway through the pastures, our headlights bouncing in the dark, revealing mounds of sleeping cattle, which on two occasions we had to skirt completely.

"We may have to shoot off the lock that goes to the hole," I said.

"No," Sandy said. "We're not going that way."

"Then where?" I asked.

"We'll do it the easy way this time," he said.

"What's that?" Larrabeth asked.

"Why, the elevator, of course," he said.

*****

It was a concrete power substation. The caliche and dirt path approaching it became smooth blacktop in the last hundred yards, and widened into a turnaround, apparently for eighteen-wheel tractor-trailer rigs.

Close by was a huge lake, its still waters reflecting the stars overhead. I had no way of knowing at that moment that in the very near future I would become extremely intimate with the water, mud and ooze from the bottom of that lake.

"This is where Bradley died," Sandy said.

"I've been wanting to see this place," I told him.

"Oh, you'll see."

We pulled up by the building and got out. The night air had stilled. Overhead there was a dazzling display of stars. The moon was down and it was terribly dark. The deputies clicked on a couple of flashlights, shined them at the black pickup that was parked there close to the door.

"Won't even need flashlights once we get inside," Sandy said. "Come on."

"Whose truck?" Larrabeth asked him.

I answered for him. I knew the truck.

"We need those suits," I told deputies Cook and Cooper.

They retrieved a large box from the trunk and set it down by the door of the building.

Beside the front door Sandy stopped and flipped up a small covering to a backlit key pad.

"I hope they haven't changed the codes," he said. "If they have and won't answer our knock, we'll have to go the long way around. As of two days ago, though, the code worked."

"What's the code?" Larrabeth asked.

"You don't have to remember any numbers," he said. "It's easier just to spell out 'gold'. That's the code."

Sandy entered the code and there was a soft *'snik'* sound and a green light by the door.

"See?" he said.

Sandy opened the door.

*****

The lights inside the substation were on, full bright. The place was air conditioned and cold. There was an enormous chiller in operation in the center of the room and a desk littered with papers, a LaserJet printer and a laptop computer. The man there stood up as we all came inside.

"Hello, Mike," I said.

"Hi, Bill. Sheriff. Brought the posse, I see. Hello, Sandy. I thought you were incommunicado."

"I got better," Sandy said.

"Then, I suppose the jig, as they say, is up."

"You're not as stupid as you were in high school," I told him.

He regarded me, smiled thinly.

"Heidi has smartened me up a bit since those days," he said.

"We're going down," Sandy said, and nodded to Larrabeth.

"Oh? Well, I won't stop you," Mike said. "But I won't help you to destroy me."

"Jim, Lawson, why don't you stay with Mr. Fields while we go down. Make sure he doesn't leave."

The deputies nodded. Their hands were on the butts of their guns.

"Am I under arrest, then?" Mike asked. "I do know a little about police procedure."

"I'm sure you do," Larrabeth said, "seeing as how your father is a Police Chief."

"Hmmm," Mike said. "I wonder if the Grimes County Sheriff knows you're investigating on his turf?"

"Maybe he doesn't," Larrabeth said. "But you see this badge?" She pointed at her chest. "It says 'State of Texas' on it."

"Point taken," Mike said. "I suppose I'd be out of line to ask to see a warrant."

Mike's question was answered by silence.

He sighed. "Well, fellahs, there's coffee over in the corner. You're welcome to help yourself."

Larrabeth rolled her eyes.

"Let's get this done," she said.

CHAPTER TWENTY-EIGHT

In 1673 a French marauder sacked and scuttled a Spanish Galleon among the Windward Islands of the Caribbean. Her captain took the treasure, a string of captives and an obscure object and ran before a hurricane toward the Texas coast. The French ship came up the Brazos River a hundred miles or more before becoming stuck in the mud, at which point her captain burned the ship and assimilated himself and his men with the natives.

The object — the 'blue bone,' as du Orly referred to it — caused madness. And in a moment of lucidity on his death bed, the captain requested as his dying wish that the blue bone be buried far beneath the land, where its curse would never again bring harm.

I had known the who and the why behind Brad's death, and I was beginning to suspect how.

Larrabeth, Sandy and I stepped into a small elevator with our overly bulky radiation suits on, and pushed the only button there: an arrow pointing down.

The elevator lurched and descended rapidly.

"Sandy," I said. "It's down there, isn't it? The treasure, the skeletons, the blue bone, everything?"

Our eyes met through the leaded glass face plates, dusty with age. There were traces of cobweb around the edge of mine.

Sandy looked away without acknowledgment.

The descent took a whole minute.

We're not so innocent.

Our actions twist in our minds and hearts and we attempt to reconcile them with our vision of who and what we are.

Sandy's guilt, though slight when compared with the person who had taken Brad's life, was still as palpable and real as if he had been responsible for many deaths.

I wondered how far I could trust Sandy. Would we have to watch him? What was he capable of? The hardest thing for a person to face is a true reflection of himself. And Sandy had yet to be forced to have a full look.

The elevator slowed at the last instant, shimmied like a dog with a fever for a moment, and came to a grinding stop. The door opened and we stepped out into a well-lit cavern, greater than a football field in length, nearly the same in width, and with a height that was staggering. The ground had been cleared of stalagmites and temporary flooring had been laid in some areas, as pathways were needed over the undulating landscape.

The center of the cavern was occupied by what could have been a blunt-nosed intercontinental ballistic missile. It was metallic blue, seamless and huge.

"What the hell is that?" Larrabeth asked.

Sandy turned to her. "It's how rich men get richer. Don't ask me how it works, 'Beth."

I touched Sandy's arm, got his attention.

"We're at least half a mile from the other site," I said. "Which is the first one you found?"

"The other one," he said. "But I found this cavern not long after during weekend spelunkings. It was Brad, doing what he called 'simple trigonometry' that figured out where to sink the elevator shaft."

"From there," I said, "all that had to be done was to put a building on top of it, and you've got your own underground laboratory."

"What does that thing really do?" Larrabeth gestured to the large object.

Sandy looked at me.

"I'll tell her," I said. "It locates radiation."

"Radiation? Our whole planet's got radiation all over it," she said. "We've been setting off atomic bombs since the forties, under the Earth, under the water, in the sky. I don't get it."

"Not the same radiation," I said. "There's a reason they had to build it underground. It's also the world's biggest lightning rod. It puts out ions by the boatload, and nature seeks to balance differences in potential. If they had built it on the surface, it would have been getting lightning strikes every time a bundle of clouds passed overhead. I found the plans in Brad's desk. It was the last place anyone would have looked for a motive for killing Freddie, to be sure. I'm not sure Freddie's actually ever read a book, much less a schematic."

"I'm lost, Bill," Larrabeth said.

"Gold," Sandy said.

"Gold? What's this about gold? You're not talking about the *Le Royale* treasure, are you?"

"Not exactly," I said. "Tell her all you know, Sandy."

He sighed, looked from her to me and then back again.

"As far as I can see, it's like this — that thing that I found, that little chest I said was haunted — it had the blue bone in it. It was the smaller version of this thing," he gestured to the large object at our backs. The thing dwarfed us. "It not only detects gold, it moves when it locks onto a good 'source', as Brad called it."

"How does it do that?"

"I don't know. That's the technical stuff." Sandy gestured to me.

"Don't look at me," I said. "I know the theory, but that's all. On Brad's tape, he talked about the original. He examined it thoroughly, put it through tests in the make-shift lab that Throckmorton set up for him back at the power plant. Brad surmised that the original was carved by the Aztecs or the Mayans or the Incas or somebody out of a piece of meteorite. It put forth questing ions of a peculiar nature, almost like a form of gravity, and these latched onto the signature of certain forms of radiation, even at a distance. But it was small and weak. Something bigger was needed."

"What's radiation have to do with gold?" Larrabeth asked.

"Gold is a very heavy element," I said. "It has a low level of radioactivity, but of a kind that's not harmful."

"Gold mines," Larrabeth said. "I've been reading up on Throckmorton and his gold mines during the last few weeks. This thing," she gestured, "accounts for his string of lucky strikes."

"Yep," Sandy said.

"Where's the treasure?" I asked Sandy. *"The Le Royale* treasure. And the original blue bone?"

"I don't know where the thing is, but the treasure is still here. It was being used for testing purposes. I'll show you."

Sandy led us along a series of planks over low pools of water and past small stalagmites, many of which had been sheared off below waist height as if they had been trees logged by heavy equipment. A series of three industrial coolers — the kind used by grocery stores to store and display ice cream — lay end to end in a small grotto to what felt to me to be the west side of the cavern. Through the glass were wooden chests. They looked ancient, yet of superior manufacture.

"This is it, huh?" I asked.

"That's all there is. Or all that's left. I took about five pounds of the gold in a croker sack and — you know what happened."

"Yeah," I said. "Where are the skeletons you mentioned?"

"There were two of them. They're in the last locker." Sandy pointed.

"Why all this?" I asked. "Why move them here? Why save the skeletons?"

"You're always asking why," Sandy said. "As far as I know the 'find', as Throckmorton called it, was to remain intact until he and Mike and Brad were done. Then, he was going to appear the big good guy by moving it all back where I originally found it and reporting it to the authorities. There would have been a complete excavation, with everything roped off and eggheads running things up at the University. Like they did with La Salle's ship *La Belle* out in Galveston bay. I heard about all that stuff until I was sick of hearing it; that's why I know."

"He was going to give it back to Texas, but only after he was finished with it himself," I said. I walked down the line and peered into the last ice cream locker. A skull grinned up at me. There were two sets of bones, arm in arm, like lovers.

"Hello, Louis," I said.

"We think the other one is his wife, left beside him years after he died," Sandy said.

Larrabeth was beside me, looking in.

The other skeleton wore beads and a leather skirt and moccasins that looked as thin as parchment.

"Now there's a love story," Larrabeth said.

"I think we've seen enough," I said.

"Right. Let's get out of here," Larrabeth said. Suddenly, even in her suit with her uniform covered, she was all Sheriff.

We turned away from the grotto and made our way back toward the elevator.

And at the moment we drew even with the large missile-like object that was the centerpiece of the cavern, the lights went out.

*****

"Shit," Larrabeth said. "Don't anybody move."

I wasn't about to. The silence was huge but for the sound of my own breathing inside the suit. It was getting furiously hot inside it and I felt lines of sweat beading up on my brow.

A yellow strobe light flashed from a metal pole close by. There was a large 'click' sound, then the whir of muted motors. The object in the center of the room began to turn.

"We're in big trouble," Sandy said.

"Where are the controls for this thing?" Larrabeth asked.

"On the surface," Sandy said. "That computer Mike was sitting in front of."

"The laptop?"

"Damn right," Sandy said. "Let's get the hell out of here."

There was just enough light from the maintenance strobe to be able to see to move, and move we did, back toward the elevator. Before we could reach it, though, the elevator car went into operation, moving upwards. We stopped in our tracks, watching it climb into shadow.

"We're under surveillance, aren't we?" I said to Sandy.

"I think so," Sandy said.

"My deputies had better be all right," Larrabeth said. "I'm gonna kill somebody if they're not."

Behind us the object continued to turn, its arc describing a sixty to seventy-foot radius.

"This is how Brad was killed, wasn't it Sandy?" I asked.

He nodded.

"I believe so," he said. "Especially now."

"When that thing points at us," I said, "we're toast."

CHAPTER TWENTY-NINE

"There's a reason," I said, hurriedly, "that they have to control it from above."

We were already in motion, moving to the right cavern wall, closer to the object but towards the rear. We left the meandering walkway of wooden planks and darted across the uneven cavern floor.

"Yeah," Sandy shouted, his voice muffled by the suit. Whenever any of us talked, it had to be at a near shout to be heard.

"Because it uses so much power," I said. "When it's going, it kills."

"Yeah," Sandy shouted back.

"Damn!" Larrabeth yelled. I looked behind me to see she had fallen down. I went back, grasped her hand and pulled her up. She had a tear in her suit at the knee. A two-inch gash. She was going to be either bleeding or badly bruised.

The massive nose of the object continued its arc towards us. I had the inkling that all we had to do was be in its general vicinity when it was discharged, and that would be it.

"I've got you," I told Larrabeth, and took her arm around my shoulder. She limped, favoring the hurt knee. It was fortunate I couldn't see her face. I didn't relish the expression of pain I knew must be there.

Sandy flashed past us. I paused and looked.

He picked up the Sheriff's gun from where it had skidded into a low pool of water.

"Come on!" he shouted, and ran ahead of us again. "The other side!"

It began as a very deep but loud hum, a sustained thing at the lowest threshold of hearing. I've heard the amplifiers of car stereos cranked up to their highest volume by kids passing by on the street late at night outside my bedroom window, and the sound is sufficiently loud to rattle the windows in their frames. This thing, though — its hum went down into my very bones.

The sound began to cycle upwards in tone.

Small pieces of cavern ceiling debris began raining down around us — small stalactites, shaken loose from their ancient roots by the terrible sound.

I brought Larrabeth around to where Sandy stood. He had the gun in front of him, finger worming its way into the trigger guard. He aimed near the base of the machine where what must be a power cable snaked upwards past a gigantic hydraulic armature.

It took no more than a glance to assess what he was trying to do. He was trying to cut the power of a four-inch cable with a .357 magnum, but directly behind that was the device that raised and lowered the object itself.

"Wait," I cried, but for the second time since I'd met him, Sandy didn't hear me. And this time, it wasn't his fault.

He fired.

*****

When things go wrong, sometimes they go badly wrong. That's been my experience, at least.

What happened after Sandy Jones fired his cousin's revolver — which made its own noise amid the cacophony of sound created by the object itself about the way a small fire-cracker might sound during a city-wide fireworks display — was out of all proportion to what could have been reasonably anticipated. And that, I believe, pretty much sums up my life.

The bullet deflected off the side of the cable and punctured a neat hole in the hydraulics system of the side we were on.

A flood of grease squirted from the hole, arcing through the air the way a male giant might relieve himself.

Sandy began backing away.

The hum from overhead increased in intensity and tone, higher in octave now, approaching Middle "C".

I pulled Larrabeth backwards, nearly stumbled and caught myself, but my eyes were glued on the lifting mechanism. As the grease spewed, the lift dropped. The object overhead began to tilt. My eyes fastened on the housing ten feet overhead that held Brad's large blue bone in place. Thin, metal straps only held it down. It had been designed such that gravity held it down and hydraulics lifted it and turned it, with the straps there as an afterthought. I took another step back. Another.

A high-pitched grating whine ensued, and this sound momentarily overcame the high-decibel production of the object itself. I watched, mesmerized, as first one, then the second metal strap snapped.

The object rolled toward us and fell.

*****

Inches.

Mere inches, and Larrabeth and I would have been crushed. We flew backwards on the shockwave and landed hard.

My faceplate cracked, a small silvery, spider's web that wove itself into being before my eyes.

Larrabeth, beside me, had her eyes glued on the spectacle unfolding before us.

An eerie glow — like that of Captain Ahab's harpoon from the old film — had formed around the blunt nose of the object as it rolled backwards, smashing the frame that once held it suspended.

It smashed the timbers beneath it, what had once covered a large depression, and butted down with a splash into the water beneath, coming to rest with its tip aimed upwards at a forty degree angle.

Fingers of lightning flashed, and then there was an explosion of bluish light that caused my eyes to reflexively close. I felt a sheet of pain behind my eyes.

And then, for only an instant, there was complete darkness and silence.

*****

I opened my eyes to the pulse of amber and a shaking in the earth.

The maintenance strobe lay on the cavern floor at my feet, now detached from the object. Whatever it had been, whatever life it had contained, was gone now. The cable that fed it was melted and fused to the rock beneath it.

Up above, on the surface, I suspected that a few cities were undergoing a brown out.

Debris threshed down from above. A chunk of stalactite fell close by on my left. And then, in the strobe flash, I saw it coming from above at the point in the cavern roof at which the object had discharged and created a gaping black hole.

An angry torrent of water came shooting down to the cavern floor.

I looked around me for some escape. There was none.

I turned in time to see Sandy struck in the head by a falling chunk of roof-rock and topple over.

I grabbed Larrabeth's outstretched arm as the wave of water rolled over us and tossed us around like the flotsam we had become.

*****

Sandy's body slammed into me and for a moment I lost my air. I was spinning beneath the water with my arm around Sandy's waist. We roiled together, slapped hard against the cavern wall and spun away again. Up, down, sideways — these became confused. My suit, however, held me up until the floor was gone.

The cavern filled. The only light source was the amber strobe, down there on the cavern floor. It flashed and danced and the sensation was that of a Halloween carnival fun house.

A glance upward and the cavern roof was twenty feet overhead.

A pallet of walkway timbers rose up between me and Larrabeth. I felt the jolt through my entire body, and wondered, briefly if I had lost part of my arm.

Larrabeth was gone.

*****

The amber strobe flashed eerily beneath the water. I felt a leak of water against my collar bone. My suit was filling with water, slowly.

In the strobe light I could make out another dark form close by me: Larrabeth. With Sandy in tow I swam to her, slowly. We were being pulled slowly toward the downward torrent of water that rapidly filled the cavern. How much water does a lake hold? Millions of gallons? Tens of millions? Large fish floated by, not level, but with heads and tails at various angles. They drifted the way shocked or dead fish might drift.

With a final kick I grasped Larrabeth's slick suit somewhere in the area of her upper back and kicked away toward what must be the rising surface.

*****

Our heads broke the surface. Above us, mere feet away, those stalactites which had withstood the shock of the explosion and not rained down on us before reflected grimly in the waning light.

I tried to peer into Sandy's glass plate, but could make out nothing but shadow. His arms floated freely.

Larrabeth's form jerked and moved in my grip. She, at least, was alive.

The torrent of water pouring into the cavern also drowned all sound. It very nearly drowned thought as well.

I knew one thing and one thing only, and this I kept in the foreground of my confused mind. The hole from which it issued was our only chance of survival.

*****

Moments passed and the water level continued to climb. Our heads bumped against the uneven roof. I tried to steady us, to keep us from being pulled into the downward rush from above and at the last moment, when I knew we would be dragged away, my chest fetched up against a narrow stalactite. I hugged it between me and Sandy with my upper body and waited.

The water climbed past my head and the pull of the torrent lessened.

The cavern was full. Likely, it would quickly drain off into the other passages Sandy had told me about — his weekend spelunking trips came to mind — and eventually find its way to the mural where a certain square-rigged ship was depicted, forever drowning it.

These were my thoughts, odd, disjointed things. I had two lives in my charge. Of this I reminded myself.

I released the stalactite and with Sandy and Larrabeth in tow in the strobing amber half-light, kicked towards the hole that must lead, somehow to the world above.

CHAPTER THIRTY

I moved in a dark world, devoid of any light.

There was, however, pressure. An intense pressure against the skin of the suit. How long had the elevator ride down to the cavern taken us? A minute? More?

The deepest caverns of which I've read are the diamond mines of South Africa, upwards to a mile beneath the Earth. A mile was over 5,000 feet. I estimated we had descended no more than several hundred feet, no more than a tenth that distance.

If that were so, then we were probably somewhere near the half-way point in the trip.

Larrabeth's suit was rapidly filling with water, this I knew from the insistent tug downwards, the buoyancy from Sandy's and my suit slowed by the iron grip of gravity and increasing weight of Larrabeth's form. I still held her with one hand and the muscles in my hand and forearm were weakening. I had one arm around Sandy's waist, holding him to me in a death grip.

As it was pitch black — there was no way to see and no way of knowing whether they were alive. I felt, though, as if we were moving upwards, slowly. The outside pressure seemed to be decreasing. Possibly we were nearing the surface.

Would we all die here in the darkness?

What a way to go. I'd at least made it home and spent some precious time with Julie and little Jennifer. Pictures of them swam in and out of my vision in the dark, a darkness that I imagined was like the blackest reaches of space.

I lost all time sense. The only thing keeping me going, keeping my legs kicking in swimmer fashion, was the ache and spasm of my muscles and the knowledge that giving up and giving in was never an option.

My head abruptly butted against something, an outcropping that felt like so much syrup. I kicked hard with my feet and dislodged my head and felt motion again.

Mud, I surmised. Lake-bottom mud around a gaping black hole that I could not see but only imagine.

I felt a jerking, a flailing against the grip of my hand that held Larrabeth's suit. She was alive, if barely so, but a coldness gripped me. It was the flail of a drowning person.

And then light, sudden, invasive. The water sheeted from my visor to reveal a hill crowned with light.

We had made it to the surface. Around us was an eerie landscape, perhaps like something from a computer-generated movie backdrop. Silvery forms flopped in the mud about us.

The lake had drained to the edge of the hole. And down there, in the dark, was a treasure trove, likely buried for all time. The water level dropped as I watched. There was little time left.

I dragged my charges to the edge of the muddy hole, inch by slow inch. I stuck Sandy into the mud there and turned all of my attention to pulling Larrabeth's inert form to the surface. I waited until the muddy syrup receded past us.

*****

Sandy was still breathing. His breath rasped and wheezed and fogged the inside of the leaded glass. I unzipped and removed his hood. He was still out cold. I left him and turned my attention to Larrabeth.

I ripped the hood away as rapidly as I could. The water had made it up to her mouth.

If she were to live I had mere moments.

I turned her head, straddled her and began pushing inward and upward below her diaphragm. Water gushed from her mouth. A small minnow dislodged from her throat and wriggled in the mud beside her head. I pushed again and more water spewed. Again I pushed. And again until no water came.

I felt of her carotid artery. Nothing.

I tilted her head back, pinched her nose between thumb and forefinger, placed my lips over hers and exhaled, watching her chest rise. The airway, at least, was clear.

Four more breaths, then I felt again.

Nothing.

I became angry.

"Goddammit," I shouted at her. "BREATHE!"

My lips again over hers, I forced more air into her lungs.

And this time I got an answer: a small, pathetic cough that meant everything.

I turned her to the side and she vomited a flood of water. I slapped her back and another volley came. She drew in a breath, a deep one, and a fit of coughing ensued.

Her eyes fluttered open. Her face contorted with pain.

"That's my girl," I whispered under my breath.

I sat there in the mud with my two patients until I felt they were out of danger.

"Bill," the voice was weak.

"Yes, Sheriff?" I said.

"See about... my deputies."

"Yes, ma'am," I replied.

I felt heavy, leaden.

At the edge of the lake I unzipped the suit and stepped out, dropping its weight in the high grass. It was fifty yards from the muddy lake shore up to the building, but still, each yard felt like a mile.

I was tired to the depths of my soul as I dragged myself up onto the truck turn-around and toward the building.

The two sheriff's cars were there, but Mike's truck was gone. Of course. I foresaw an interesting encounter between the two of us in the future.

The sky had paled to the east with the coming dawn.

I tapped in the code by the front door, spelling out "gold" on the keypad.

The door clicked as the small green light winked on.

*****

Inside, Jim Cook and Lawson Cooper, Larrabeth's deputies, were out like a light. Their forms were sprawled on the hard concrete floor of the building. Each breathed, shallowly. Each had a knot on his head where they had made not a light contact with the floor. I was concerned enough about them to fish out my cell phone and dial 911. After a minute of wrangling with the dispatcher, trying to give her adequate directions, I was informed help was on the way.

I was beginning to feel woozy and so opened the only door to the outside and propped it open with one of the boxes that had contained the anti-radiation suits. I breathed in the night air, filling my lungs, and my head began to clear. There was a strange taste on my tongue, sort of like burnt onions. I'd have to look that one up later, but from all appearances the deputies had been somehow gassed.

I went back inside and pulled the deputies to the open doorway, one at a time, then fished in Jim Cooper's pocket until I came up with a set of keys.

"Jim," I whispered softly to his sleeping form, "I have to borrow your squad car."

CHAPTER THIRTY-ONE

Full morning. It had been an hour since I pulled Sheriff Larrabeth Williams and Sandy Jones from the mud of the bed of a former lake. I'd passed the entourage of sirens and flashing lights along Highway 30 into town, rolling on past in Jim Cook and Lawson Cooper's patrol vehicle unmolested.

I pulled up in front of the house at 7:40 a.m.

The front door was unlocked. I went inside.

No lights were on, but the sunlight filtering in from the living room windows was enough for me to see clearly.

"Hello?" I called out. "Anybody home?"

No answer. I felt a familiar chill.

I wandered into the living room. I parted the curtains an inch and peered into the back yard.

Mike was sitting there at his picnic table, sipping a longneck beer and surrounded by his beautiful Japanese tea garden. A spray of apricot blossoms was suspended a few feet over his head.

I went through the living room and peered into Mike's den. There was a desk there.

I sifted through the papers there. Nothing of importance to matters at hand.

The second door was a bathroom, its interior dark.

The third door was Mike and Heidi's bedroom, deserted.

I went in and began going through dressers, nightstands.

At the top of Heidi's clothes closet, underneath a layer of fresh linens, I found what I was looking for.

I heard something in the hallway. My hand, holding it, went behind my back.

I turned.

Heidi stood there between me and her bedroom door, regarding me.

*****

"It was storming that night," I said. "The night that Freddie died. The same night Sandy took me down into the hole."

"Yes," she said.

"And you had it with you. The blue bone. You came on to him. You propositioned him in Mary Jo's house."

She nodded.

"And you had sex with him on Mary Jo's bed. That's why he was naked. His clothes were off *before* he was dead, not after. You probably killed him at the moment of his goddamned climax."

She smirked at me, her lips drawing up into a widening grin. There was a touch of something there that I never thought I'd actually see but that I knew must exist. I'd known it from the moment I'd played Brad's tape. It was the same thing I'd seen on the faces of people who were behind bars, permanently. A species of insane glee.

"And you did it with this," I said, and brought the object up from behind my back where she could see it.

She laughed.

"I know," I said. "The resemblance to a sex toy wasn't lost on you."

The silence in her room stretched out. I threw the thing on her bed.

"It was you that night in that dark house. I thought it was a man. I knew it couldn't be Mike. He followed me and Mary Jo into town and took the turn-off to go home, to you. After Freddie was dead, you set the traps for me — the chair, the lamp. Then you went outside, threw the power switch and came back in tracking mud everywhere with Mike's boots that are in your closet there with the dried mud still on them. And then you waited. You knew I'd be bringing Mary Jo back home. But with the house so dark, you knew I'd come in first, that I wouldn't let her in without making sure she would be safe. You were playing with me."

She chuckled. I felt the chill again, and knew I was right.

"You killed Freddie with that thing," I continued. "Before that, you killed Brad the same way. I have his confession for his misdeeds on a tape. You're likely going to prison, Heidi. Or an asylum."

"You think I'm insane," she said. She laughed again, a wild and mad laugh that sent chills down my spine.

"Bill Travis," she said. "The man who thinks he's God. Well, let's see how much a god can take. Yes, I made love to Brad, just like I did with Sandy and Terry. I needed Brad. I wanted him to call you. I wanted you in on this with me. We could have had anything, everything we wanted together. The wealth of nations, the creature comforts afforded by an army of our own servants. My way to you was through him. But he was loyal to you, Bill. That's what killed him. At first I saw him as an opportunity. He was so goddamned smart. Mike says that he was decades ahead of his time. He was. His designs built the Dowser. With it we were able to locate gold deposits throughout the world, from one remote location without going *anywhere*. But Brad was in the way all along. He was between you and me, Bill. He had to die, don't you see that? So that we could build a future... together."

"You killed Brad with his own invention," I said. "You brought his dead body back up to the surface and tried to make it look like an accident. But Mike knew. And Sandy knew. They both thought Terry Throckmorton killed Brad. That put Mike in a horrible position — his own boss the killer of his best friend. You set your own husband up. You're a liar *and* a murderer, Heidi."

The effect was that of a slap. Her head rocked back slightly. Then her eyes narrowed and fixed on me with an intensity. A hatred, possibly. I decided she deserved another slap.

"And a whore," I said. "You sold your own soul."

"You have no idea what I sold," she said.

She reached up and pulled at her hair. A wig came off her head to reveal a completely smooth scalp.

"I have cancer," she said. "Inoperable. I'm dying. I won't last another year. Your prison and your asylum don't frighten me at all, Bill."

"The radiation," I said quietly. "You went down there without protection. Mike didn't know you were going down there. Sandy didn't know either. It was all you. But you had to have a confederate, or you couldn't have gone down there at all. You didn't have a key and you didn't have the codes."

She stood there, looking at me. The wig tumbled to the floor. She appeared so small, so frail to me. When I had first appeared at her front door on a day that seemed like a lifetime ago, I had noted how frail she looked.

"Throckmorton," I said. "He had the keys to the kingdom. I can see it now. Mike whispering to you in the night after a long day at work, telling you things he shouldn't have told anyone. And you began to formulate a plan. But Throckmorton had the last laugh. He didn't warn you about the core rods. You wouldn't have known what they were. He trusted you about as much as you trusted him. But you two were sleeping with each other anyway. Then you sent him to Sandy's house that night, the same night you killed Freddie."

I stood there, regarding her, watching her face and seeing silent acknowledgment there for everything I was saying to her. Also, I was looking at the pictures flitting through my head. That night. That dark night of rain and intense lightning. Mary Jo and Sandy and Dottie, their kids there.

"Sandy had his shotgun within easy reach," I said. "You set Throckmorton up and you set Sandy up to be ready when he came. You're responsible for that death as well, and for Sandy's guilt. All that in one night. My God, Heidi. You're evil. Cancer — the slow way — is just too good for you."

CHAPTER THIRTY-TWO

I wasn't expecting it. That's how bad things usually happen.

Heidi threw herself at me. Her arms went around me and she kissed my lips, furiously. Her arms were locked and her face pressed hard against mine.

I twisted, turned my head away from her.

"Don't say 'no', Bill. God how I want you. All my life I've wanted you. I've dreamed about you. When Mike made love to me it was you, Bill. It was you thrusting into me."

"Heidi!" I yelled. "Stop!"

She continued to wrestle with me, her lips burrowing hotly against my neck, her tongue snaking up to my ear where her pleas softened. She breathed into my ear, like a lover.

I grasped her arms and pulled them away with all my strength.

I pushed her away from me with all that I could muster and she fell backward onto the bed.

"NO!" she cried, and burst into tears.

"You don't love me, Bill! You never loved me! You LIED."

"I did love you," I said softly. "Once."

I hardened myself for the next volley, the one that I hoped would sink her for good and all.

"Once was enough, Heidi."

She broke down into the most mournful wail I'd ever heard from a woman's throat. A death wail.

I turned and walked out her bedroom door, closing it behind me.

I thought I was done. I was certain it was all through. I would go to my car, get in it, and go to the nearest police station and there lay everything out nice and neat.

I never got the chance.

"Wait, Bill," the softest of voices said behind me down the hallway to the living room.

I turned.

The gun was aimed at my chest.

"Don't be stupid, Heidi," I said.

She smiled through her tears. Her face was flushed red. She had the wig back on and the tresses were bedraggled. Her smile spoke volumes on the subject of women scorned and madness. What was the saying? I couldn't recall it at the moment.

"Stupid," she said. "That's me. That's my whole life. I loved you, Bill, ever since that day in high school you walked away and didn't want me anymore. How's that for stupid? My best friend used to say that I wouldn't have a man that would have me. God, that is too true."

"I'm sorry for you, Heidi," I said.

"You're dead, Bill. Like your stupid friend Brad Fisher. He didn't want me either. I only wanted him as a way to you. You left, Bill. You left my world and you left me here, alone. I've been dying Bill. At first it was a feeling in my soul. A numbness. A going away. Now it's real. The cancer is real. I said I'd be dead before the year is gone. Now I see it's a good thing."

The gun leveled at me never wavered. Pretty soon, mere seconds now, perhaps, she was going to shoot.

"Heidi," I whispered. "Don't."

Then I felt the other presence behind me, brushing by me. A shadow, passing.

Mike.

"Stop, Mike!" she shouted.

He came to an abrupt halt.

"What're you going to do?" he asked. "Shoot Bill? Why? Because he rebuffed you, just like all the other men? Like Brad? Sleeping with them wasn't good enough? You had to own them."

It was my second time to be shocked. Mike knew. Mike, the man who knows everything. I'd once made him plow up the high school lawn with his face.

"No," she said. "Not like Brad. Not at all like Brad."

"Bill," Mike said, his back still to me, "I wouldn't let her kill you when you were in the hole, and I won't let her do it now. I'm sorry, Bill. I can't control my wife. I never could."

"Shut up, Mike!" Heidi shouted. "You're a worthless piece of crap. And you're in my *way!*"

"I never was much of a man," Mike said. Possibly he was talking to himself. "But I'm becoming one. This is where I make my stand. You can't kill him, Heidi. By God, I won't let you."

Heidi laughed. "You're right, Mike," she said. "I can't shoot Bill." Her voice now no more than a whisper again, and I shivered.

"That's right," Mike said. "You're not so stupid after all."

"Wrong," she replied. "I can shoot *you.*"

The report was the loudest thing I have ever heard.

The tall, bear-like figure before me fell backwards into my arms.

CHAPTER THIRTY-THREE

Who knows the twisted byways of the human heart?

Who knows what it is capable of?

Louis du Orly knew, perhaps. Brad Fisher may have had a clue when he warned Mary Jo not to call me for help. Mike Fields, I believed, was constitutionally incapable of knowing. He suffered from his own particular malady — he loved a woman who could not return his love. And now he was suffering for it, in the worst way a man can suffer. He was fighting for his life.

I watched the ER team go to work on him, his chest bare, blood congealing around a jagged hole.

The curtain was pulled, thankfully, and my view was cut off.

Mike might make it out alive, and doing so might be the roughest part for him.

*****

All my days I have searched for an answer to the question: "What makes people do things that will bring them misery and pain?" One author I had read hit if not *it,* then closest to it than anyone ever had before when he said something to the effect that a man has to have his life threatened several times a day or he feels as though he's not really alive. I suppose he was right, in light of what I had found out about Brad and Mike and Heidi. How that author figured that out, I'll never know. For me it seems to be the air knifing through my lungs, the too-bright glint of something coming my way, and even the coming darkness and the long hours before the dawn. Something, seemingly even something bad, as it were, is always better than nothing at all. I believe that holds true for everyone, myself included.

*****

On my way out of the ER, I dropped in on Jim Cook and Lawson Cooper. They had a contingent of Sheriff's deputies surrounding them and getting in the way of the nursing staff. At first I had difficulty getting through them, then Cooper saw me and waved me on in.

"I've heard you may have saved my life," he said.

"Nothing that dramatic. I just opened the door and got you to some good air. Tell me what happened?"

Jim laughed, but then rubbed his temple in obvious pain.

"It was a woman," he said. "The wife of that guy we were watching. Small, thin woman —"

"I know her," I said.

"Thought she was harmless. She had a squirt gun with her. A kid's toy. Hell, when she pointed it me, I laughed. She laughed too. Then she squirted me in the face and my lights went out."

"What do you think it was?" I asked.

"Chloroform," Lawson Cooper said. He was on his feet now, albeit a trifle wobbly. "Did they get her?" he asked.

"She's in custody," I said.

"Good," he said. "Bitch."

"Yep," I agreed.

I spent the better part of the day with Larrabeth Williams at the hospital and met her family. I hadn't known that she was married and the mother of two nearly grown boys. Each one hugged me tightly and thanked me for her life.

Outside the hospital window I could see news vans setting up to broadcast. They began to take up a significant portion of the visitor parking area and I watched with passing interest. At one point there appeared to be a heated exchange between a hospital administrator and a news reporter. I knew I'd be locating an alternate exit when the time came for me to disappear.

"Where are you off to now, Bill?" Larrabeth asked from her hospital bed as I inched my way to the door, preparatory to leaving.

"I've got a broken window to fix."

*****

That night I put myself up at the same hotel I'd stayed in during my previous trip and was awakened with the dawn by a cell phone call from the Texas Rangers. They wanted to talk. Go figure.

Sandy was there at the county courthouse when I arrived. I was thankful he wasn't in irons. He'd given his statement and was on his way out in the company of the Texas Ranger I'd come to talk with. Sandy still had a bandage over his head. Likely, he'd spent the better portion of the night telling his story.

We paused before passing each other.

"Dottie knows I slept with Heidi Fields," he said. "I shouldn't have done it, blackmail or no blackmail."

"You and Dottie gonna be all right?" I asked.

"I think so," he said and rubbed the bandage over his brow. "Thank God I nearly got killed! It was the only thing that saved me from Dottie killing me when I told her. And if she was going to, I figured the best place to do it was at the hospital. I'm not joking, Bill."

"I know."

Sandy looked down at his feet. I waited.

"I suppose," he said, "I've got some heavy-duty amends to make. Not only to my woman, but to my kids. I think even maybe on my job."

I couldn't help smiling.

"I'm not so sure I like seeing you this way," I said.

"What do you mean?" he asked.

"All contrite. Where you are is just in a condition. A lower condition, mind you, than that of the trusted and benevolent husband and father, but it's still just a condition. Recognize it for what it is and just do something about it. But blaming yourself? Maybe it makes it feel a little better for you, but it never works, at least not for long."

Sandy smiled slowly at me and chuckled.

"All right," he said. "All right."

"How did you come by your nickname?" I asked. "'Sandy'."

"Stealing watermelons as a boy," he said. "Once when the owner of this watermelon patch lit after us, all the other kids ran. One of my cousins got caught and got the tar whaled out of her. Me, I dropped to the ground and covered myself up with dirt and sand. When I got home I still had sand coming out of my ears. The name stuck from that day forward."

"Who got caught?" I asked.

"I call her 'Beth. You'd just call her 'Sheriff'."

We both laughed.

I extended my hand. He took it and shook hard.

"Thanks, Bill," he said. "I owe you. For everything."

"You owe me dinner and a game of Monopoly with your family," I said.

The Texas Ranger shook hands with Sandy and gave him his calling card, then Sandy walked out of the Courthouse.

And then it was my turn.

*****

I brought in Brad's tape and played it for the Ranger. The tape alone took the better part of an hour. I'd heard it all before, and did my best to ponder other things and not focus in on Brad's haunting voice.

The tape detailed Sandy's discovery of the hole and the treasure, Terry Throckmorton's use of Brad's talents as an engineer in discovering the uses of the ancient device and his suppositions on its composition and how it worked. It was Brad's contention that it was shaped from a piece of meteorite that had contained trace elements of several heavy metals, including one that is designated with a question mark on old periodic element charts. The closest thing to it in "harmonic," as he described it, was plutonium. That was the 'why' behind the core rods to begin with. Brad went on to detail the machinations of Heidi Fields and how he had given in to her, as Sandy had. If I could have spoken with Brad, just once, I would have talked him out of the whole thing, his tryst with Heidi especially. Once a person's integrity goes, the sinking is as quick and as inevitable as a ship hulled below the water line. In the final analysis, that's all integrity is: knowing what is right and then doing it.

The tape done, I passed the journal across the table. The Ranger leafed through it slowly for a minute, then slid it back to me across the wide table.

"What are you going to do with it?" he asked me.

"I thought maybe it belongs in a museum."

He nodded.

"It's an environmental disaster," I said. "It has to be cleaned up."

"I know," he said. "When the water level drops down there, we'll have the feds go in. They have ecological disaster-type people who can handle this kind of thing in their sleep."

I hadn't thought of that. The cave system had little pools dotting its eerie, otherworldly landscape. Nothing more. It was certain the water would recede.

"Sounds like the Corps of Engineers will have to fix that lake," I said.

"No doubt," the Ranger intoned, and yawned.

"Are you going to be there for the cleanup?" I asked him.

"Shoot. I hope not," he said.

"Then can you pass the word along?"

"What word?"

"About the treasure. There's a treasure-trove down there in the dark."

"Oh. Yeah. I forgot. I'll handle it."

The conversation lapsed. I expected him to stand, but instead he thumped his pencil eraser on a legal note pad and looked at me expectantly.

"What happens to Heidi Fields?" I asked him. It was, perhaps, the main question of the day.

He sighed. "She's going to the Rusk State Hospital for the Criminally Insane at the very least. It'll be a voluntary committal. I've already spoken with her about it. She says she's dying. I believe her. She'll never go to trial. Wouldn't be any point."

He waited. I had a feeling that twisted in my guts. There was something this fellow needed to hear, and I hadn't covered it yet.

Then it hit me.

"Sandy Jones told you everything, didn't he? And by everything, I mean *all.*"

He nodded.

"I didn't shoot Throckmorton. That one was a given. Is he going to be arrested and tried?"

The Ranger shook his head slowly.

"He'll walk on that one, and on everything else," he said.

The knot in my stomach loosened. That was it, as far as I was concerned.

The Ranger smiled. "I just wanted to hear you say it. You had a friend of mine pretty-well fooled."

"Oh," I said. "The Grimes County Sheriff. Sorry about that."

"I'll settle it with him," he said.

"Then my thanks are due," I said.

He pushed his chair back and regarded me.

"Can you deliver a message for me?" I asked.

"Sure."

"It's to Heidi."

He nodded.

"Tell her I'll never forget her. And I forgive her."

What is a fellow supposed to feel at such a time? I wasn't sure. Still, I felt something. It wasn't a sad thing, nor the empty feeling I've had so many times before during my life. I thought back to a certain look, a certain glint in Heidi's eye from years gone by — a lifetime ago. And then I knew. It was a sense of loss all right, but only of opportunity. What had occurred to precipitate these events, or, better, what had not occurred that would have, perhaps, averted it? I was never much into self-blame, but reflecting on it there under the steely-eyed yet bored stare of a Texas Ranger, the words of an over-used poem came to mind, and it was too right not to fit. I had taken a different road, a diverging path less-traveled, and that had made all the difference.

"I have something for you," the Ranger said.

"What?"

He reached into the leather case beside his chair and slid it across the table to me.

I looked at it. Its smooth surface reflected the overhead fluorescent lighting.

"What am I supposed to do with that?" I asked.

"I don't care," he said. "I don't like it. I don't want it anywhere near me."

"And you don't need it?" I said. Of course he didn't.

He shook his head slowly.

I pushed my own chair back. We stood, shook hands, and that, as they say, was that.

*****

On the way to the parking lot opposite the courthouse, I dropped the thing in the county refuse bin. It landed with a loud plop on top of a pile of discarded jailhouse food. The box from which the stuff oozed bore a label that read, 'Vanilla Pudding.' The sign on the bin said, 'Official Use Only — Penalty.'

Which was about perfect.

*****

I drove east across town, out of my way, and dropped du Orly's journal in the return slot at the local natural history museum with a brief note that read:

Circa 1670 - 1683. The real life adventure of a French explorer who found friends, peace, and a final resting place in Texas.

I didn't bother to sign my name.

*****

Before leaving town I made a phone call to the Bryan Police Department. I asked if Harvey Leonard was on patrol. He was. I asked the dispatcher to relay a message to him and gave it.

I waited there at the Shell gas station at the corner of 25th and Texas Avenue.

Seven minutes later the patrol car pulled in behind me. I got out, walked back to Officer Leonard's window.

He rolled his window down, looked up at me.

"Will you take off those damned sunglasses?" I asked him.

He removed them, looked up at me with steely-gray eyes.

"Yeah? So?"

"She's dying, Harvey," I said. "They're taking her to Rusk."

It appeared there was a bone in his throat. He swallowed, hard. His lips tightened. He rolled his window up, put his car in gear and eased past mine and was off into traffic, accelerating away.

EPILOGUE

The drive back to Austin was filled with a dramatic sunset, the like of which I don't believe I have witnessed before. The leading edge of a bank of intensely white and fluffy clouds piled mountainously high was limned with brilliant orange light much like permanent lightning, a product of the brilliant rays from a fading sun. All of this tapered away into a forever deep blue sky and presented an upside down landscape, the reflection of an Earth that might have been in some primordial time stream. It was the sort of scene that fantasy artists have always tried earnestly to capture, and have always, always fallen short. I've heard it said that when we have sunsets like that, that volcanoes are going off somewhere in the world, that it's really just dust and soot and strange elements in the atmosphere filtering the dying sunlight, doing strange things to it. One could think that way — and I usually have to catch myself and yank myself back from thinking that way when I find myself doing so — but I'd like to think instead that it was a sunset heralding a new night and a new day beyond. And, hopefully, a sea change of some kind. A change not in the weather, but in the world, or at the very least, in my world.

Before the trip was done I found myself drifting through memory. I revisited Heidi as I had known her all those years before. I dropped in on Brad and Mary Jo, had a few beers and a few laughs. Sandy and Dottie and their kids welcomed me into their little home, and this time I lost heavily at Monopoly to a smiling child. Sheriff Williams and her deputies and her family had a barbecue picnic together in my mind, and I was welcome at their table. We drank longneck beer and talked about county politics. And then, as I parted company with each one in turn, I began looking ahead as the miles passed and all evidence of the sun disappeared, toward a future beautiful and terrible. What might it discover in what strange lands?

I found my way home after a time, to my wife and my new baby. And when I came into our room and found mother and daughter together and the little one grasped my finger in her oh so tiny ones and gave me a very large smile, I knew that living would be taking on far more meaning than it ever had before.

AUTHOR'S NOTE

Louis du Orly and his ill-fated ship and crew are entirely a product of this author's imagination, and to my knowledge, no such adventure occurred in actual history. But calculate, if you will, how many ships in history never made it home to port and you can see that the events I have described here are entirely possible, especially given the treacherous nature of the mid-Atlantic and the Gulf of Mexico.

I knew a Heidi in high school, a year ahead of me, but this Heidi is not that Heidi by any means. I've always liked the name.

Brad Fisher is a composite of many friends, old and new, as is his wife, Mary Jo.

I don't know where Mike Fields came from. What author truly knows where his characters come from? But that question, of course, is purely rhetorical.

I hope Officer Harvey Leonard is fictitious.

The power company in this book is fictitious, as are each and every character associated with it.

The counties and cities as given here are real. However, Brazos County does not have a black female Sheriff, nor has it ever had one to my knowledge. I wouldn't mind seeing that changed in the future. Likewise, I have never met the Sheriff of Grimes County.

The hole is fictitious. To my knowledge, such does not exist. There are, however, dark places, unknown and seemingly unknowable, deep down there beneath us all. A world of staggering beauty if light were to find it and eyes were to see it. If these, however, are not indeed real, then they are at least real in my mind.

Human nature is the most difficult thing for any author to accurately portray, as we are insubstantial beings and our thoughts are our own possessions, impenetrable to the end. I have attempted at every turn to put into words the impressions I have sensed from the many people I have known throughout my life. For me, these characters live and breathe, but that is only right. If it were not so, then the error would be of the greatest magnitude.

Sometimes I feel as though my mind is like so much clay, there for the world to indelibly impress its imagery and subtle nuances. In this way, life for this author is rich surpassing any treasure of the ancient world. And that, in the final analysis, is the only thing which I can truly share with you, reader. My friend. My treasure is your treasure.

George Wier
Austin, Texas

Read the prologue and first chapter of George Wier's next thrilling *Bill Travis Mystery*:

THE DEVIL TO PAY

Coming soon

PROLOGUE

Phil Burnet retired as curator from the Texas Ranger Museum in Waco, Texas on his sixty-third birthday having filed early for his social security benefit. His mind was made up to settle down and do what he had for thirty-five years sworn before God and family he would do: fish all day, every day, until he died. He had proclaimed on more than one occasion that when they found his dead body with his old cane-pole in his stiff hand, they shouldn't bother trying to remove it, but instead weight his body down and shove him on into the water. He'd be much happier that way and it would balance the books between him and the Texas Parks and Wildlife Department for all the fish he was to have taken during the intervening years, for which he had planned on the round number of forty — forty years of catching, cleaning and frying his own supper. His grandfather had lived to be 102, and he was aiming to best him.

Phil Burnet went fishing that first Saturday after his retirement dinner and was never seen alive again.

*****

The Colorado River is a thoroughly dammed and level-controlled waterway after it meanders its way down from the high North Texas plains to become Lake Travis. Below the lake's broad dam is a spillway where the waters again begin to resemble a very broad river that snakes its way for miles through West Austin suburbs for the upwardly mobile and affluent in the high hills to become what is locally known as Town Lake, recently renamed Lady Bird Lake after President Johnson's widow.

The waterway and shores of Town Lake have been sculpted over time into a large city park with stands of native trees, hike and bike trails and picnic areas, much of the funding for which was gleaned through the influence of the long-lived former president's wife.

On a Saturday afternoon, exactly one week to the day after his first and final foray into his retirement pastime and at a time optimum for city residents to enjoy the tranquil lake, Phil Burnet put in an appearance again. Phil Burnet was thoroughly dead. Dead did not come much deader.

The discovery of the body was ultimately attributed to one Perry Reilly, a local, who had taken his canoe and his new young and beautiful insurance associate out onto the water for a little "quality time." Perry was a womanizer. This he knew and couldn't help. His father had been a womanizer. His grandfather had raised three different families during three different eras, and if family rumors were true, had fathered other children that did not show up on the family tree charts kept by the estimable elderly family hens. So, for Perry Reilly, the blue blood had run true. Angela Thompson was beautiful, she was unattached, she was an associate, and she was twenty-five years his junior, which, according to Perry's moral compass, made her fair game.

He was alternating his paddle strokes along Barton Creek toward Town Lake and occasionally pointing at something on either bank in order to distract Angela long enough to hopefully catch a fleeting glance near where her legs joined beneath cotton athletic shorts and the brownish shadows began there in the narrow gaps. Angela Thompson wore baggy clothing when not in the office. It was the style, and today Perry approved.

Angela peered into the waters, intently.

"Perry. Stop. Hold a sec."

"What is it?" he asked. He had almost added a 'Darling' on the end of his question, but training took hold and saved him.

"It's... Tell me what that is." Her voice had become no more than whisper. Her brows frowned, her eyes squinted. She pointed.

"Lean back for a second. We both can't look at the same time. This thing will tip over."

She looked away, opposite side, and closed her eyes.

Perry looked over the side and saw something down there: eight, ten feet down, possibly more. The shadows and the light did strange things in deep water. Shapes melded and blended and anything could look like anything, this he knew. But he also knew that what he was seeing was what was there.

He swore under his breath.

There was movement for a moment down there, an upward drift of something. It looked like a hand with a single extended finger, pointing at him in accusation.

"Perry?" Angela said, distress in her voice. He looked. Her eyes were still shut and she was squeezing them tight.

"Hush, now," he said.

There was a quick flick of motion down there and something black and round darted away toward the shadows beneath the trees overhanging the wide creek. A turtle. Biggest mother he had ever seen. The lake was full of the beggars.

Perry Reilly then did the bravest thing he had ever done in his entire life. He reached into his shirt pocket and removed his cellular phone.

"I gotta make a call," he said.

CHAPTER ONE

Walt Cannon stopped by my office on a Sunday morning at about the same moment that the portal gates of hell opened up and black things began slithering forth.

My name is Bill Travis. I've got a home and a wife full of children and have no business with trouble, or at least I shouldn't. I could have tried telling that to Walt Cannon and a lot of good it would have done me.

"I need your help, Bill," Walt said.

"Have a seat, Walt," I said, knowing I shouldn't. Walt is likable, though. He's a lean and muscled fellow, a tad over six feet in height and carries an air of authority about him even when he isn't in uniform, which at the moment he was. Looking at Walt's face is like looking back a century into the seamed face of an Old West cattle drover. In his younger years Walt would have made a good Marlboro Man.

"What's the trouble?" I asked.

And so he laid it out about Phil Burnet and his retirement and his vanishment and return. Perry Reilly's name came up when I asked who had found him.

"Perry's my business neighbor," I said. "The insurance office right next door."

"Right," Walt said. "I didn't even think about you, Bill, until I walked out of his office and looked this way. It's been a while."

"It's been forever," I said, remembering a certain barbecue beneath the metal sculpture of a Tyrannosaurus Rex at Walt's West Texas ranch.

"A lot happens in a few years."

"That's all too true. Why me, Walt? I can get my partner Nat to keep your books, maybe even cook 'em —" I looked at his face. "Just kidding," I said. "But really, why me? I don't have a license to investigate. Legally, I can't even ask questions. What gives?"

"Because," he said, and paused. "First, it's not my investigation. It's being handled by the locals as a simple murder case, even though any Ranger has, by tradition, jurisdiction anywhere in the state. On this one I dare not go very far myself."

"Then why were you talking to Perry?" I asked.

He sighed, uncrossed his legs and shifted in his chair. This was it. The mule was about to get the two-by-four right between the eyes. I leaned back in my chair and stared at him across my disheveled desk.

Walt looked at his hands. They were reddish, rough and leathery. His knuckles appeared to have knuckles.

"I didn't know what else to do," he said, and I allowed the silence that followed to linger. I wasn't about to speak.

"Bill, there are some folks in the Ranger Service that are pretty sure... They think... Aw hell. Might as well spit it out. They think I killed Phil Burnet."

*****

I remembered one time Walt telling me about a kid who had said to him: "I heard you're a Texas Ranger." Walt replied: "That's right," to which the kid replied with a damning question: "What position do you play?"

There's little romance in any line of work. A job, I have found, is a job. But for some men and women their job is their life. That's what I was thinking about when I asked Walt Cannon the question that no one else I know would have been brazen enough to ask: "Did you, Walt? Did you kill him?"

"No," he said slowly, if 'no' can be said slowly. "But I would have. I sure as hell wanted to."

And then somewhere I felt a black door opening.

"I suppose," I said, "you need to tell me more about Phil Burnet."

CPSIA information can be obtained at www.ICGtesting.com
Printed in the USA
LVOW11s1939070814

398029LV00008B/996/P